Fairy Dust
and the
Quest for the Egg

GAIL CARSON LEVINE

Fairy Dust and the Quest for the Egg

ILLUSTRATED BY
DAVID CHRISTIANA

HarperCollins *Children's Books*

First published in the USA by Disney Press, 114 Fifth Avenue,
New York New York 10011-5690.

First published in Great Britain in 2005 by HarperCollins
Children's Books. HarperCollins Children's Books is a division of
HarperCollinsPublishers, 77 - 85 Fulham Palace Road,
Hammersmith, London W6 8JB.

The HarperCollins website address is:
www.harpercollinschildrensbooks.co.uk

Text by Gail Carson Levine. Art by David Christiana.
Copyright © 2005 Disney Enterprises, Inc. All rights reserved.

0-00-720929-0

1 2 3 4 5 6 7 8 9 10

Printed and bound in Clays Ltd. St Ives plc

Visit disneyfairies.com

Fairy Dust and the Quest for the Egg

*W*HEN BABY Sara Quirtle laughed for the first time, the laugh burbled out of her and flitted through her window. It slid down the side of her house and pranced along her quiet lane. It took a right on Water Street, and frolicked on to the wide sea that separated the mainland from Neverland. There the laugh set out, skipping from the tip-top of one wave to the tip-top of the next.

But after two weeks of dancing over the ocean, the laugh veered too far to the south. It would have missed the island entirely if Neverland hadn't moved south, too. The island was looking for the laugh.

The fact is, you can't find Neverland if it doesn't want you, and if it does want you, you can't miss it.

The island is an odd place. The humans (or Clumsies, as the fairies call them) and the animals who live there never grow old. Never. That's why the island is called Neverland.

The only reason the island rides the waves is because Clumsy children believe in it. If a time ever comes when they all lose faith, Neverland will lift up and fly away. Even now, if a single Clumsy child stops believing in fairies, a Never fairy dies — unless enough Clumsy children clap to show that they believe.

Sometimes the island is huge, and sometimes it's small. Its inhabitants mostly live near the shore. The forests and the plains and Torth Mountain, where the dragon Kyto is imprisoned, are largely unexplored.

As soon as the island moved, Mother Dove knew a laugh was on its way. High time, she thought. She felt lucky whenever a new arrival was coming. And the fairies would be jubilant.

She told Beck, the finest animal-talent fairy in Neverland. Beck told her friend Moth, who could light the entire Home Tree with her glow. Moth told Tinker Bell and eight other fairies.

You see, when a baby laughs for the first time, the laugh turns into a fairy. Often it turns into a mainland fairy — a Great Wanded fairy or a Lesser Wanded fairy or a Spell-Casting fairy or a Giant Shimmering fairy. Occasionally it turns into a Never fairy.

Word spread to all the talents. Each one wanted the new fairy, and each one made an extra effort to deserve her. The keyhole-design-talent fairies whipped up a dozen fresh designs. The caterpillar-herders found a caterpillar that had been missing for a week. And the music-talent fairies, who had just lost a fairy to disbelief, practised an extra hour every day.

Approaching the island, the laugh slipped under a mermaid's rainbow. It breezed by the pirate ship in Pirate Cove, too silly to be scared. When it touched shore, it sped up and hurtled along the beach, not even pausing to admire the flock of giant yellow-shelled tortoises.

The laugh shrank and became more concentrated. After it passed the fifty-fourth conch shell, it canted inland. It hadn't gone far, however, before the air hardened against it. The laugh was forced to slow down to a crawl.

The trouble was that Neverland was having doubts. This laugh was a little different, and the island wasn't sure whether to let it in.

Below lay Fairy Haven. Fairies were flying in and out of the their rooms in the Home Tree, a towering maple that is the heart of Fairy Haven. Fairies were washing windows, taking in laundry, watering windowsill flowerpots – making everything shipshape in honor of the evening's celebration of the Molt.

The laugh sensed it belonged down there. It tried to descend, but it couldn't.

In the lower stories of the Home Tree, fairies were busy in their workshops. Two sewing-talent fairies were rushing to finish an iris-petal gown. Bess, the island's foremost artist, was putting the finishing touches on a portrait of Mother Dove.

If Bess – or any of the others – had known the laugh was overhead, she'd have flown out her window and helped it along. She'd have called more fairies to help too. And they'd have come, every single one – even nasty Vidia, even dignified Queen Clarion.

On the tree's lowest story, fairies bustled about the kitchen, unaware of the laugh. Two cooking-talent fairies hefted a huge roast of mock turtle into the oven. Three sparrow men (male fairies) argued over the best way to slice the night's potato. And a baking-talent fairy consulted with a coiffure-talent fairy over the braiding of the bread.

Above, the laugh pushed on, fighting for every inch.

It passed above the oak tree that was the Home Tree's nearest neighbour. The laugh had no idea that a crew of scullery-talent fairies was working under the tree. Protected by nutshell helmets, they were collecting acorns for tonight's soup.

In the barnyard beyond the oak tree, four dairy-talent fairies milked four dairy mice. The fairies failed to see the laugh's faint shadow as it crossed over each mouse's back.

In the orchard on the other side of Havendish Stream, a squad of fruit-talent fairies picked two dozen cherries for two dozen cherry pies. If only they'd looked up!

The laugh reached the edge of Fairy Haven where Mother Dove sat, as always, on her egg in the lower branches of a hawthorn tree. The nest was next to the fairy circle, where tonight's celebration would be held.

Did the laugh feel the pull of Mother Dove's goodness? I don't know, but it bunched itself for a final effort.

If Mother Dove hadn't been distracted, she'd have felt the laugh. But she was listening as a fairy recited her lines for a skit tonight, and she was watching as another fairy practised her flying polka. Mother Dove wanted to nod encouragingly to them, but she had to keep her head still so Beck could tie a ribbon around her neck.

Overhead, the laugh pushed with all its might. At the same moment, Neverland decided to let it in.

It spun once, then zoomed faster and faster, above Mother Dove, back over the orchard, past the mice and the oak tree, on a downward course. It achieved final sneeze force and exploded right outside the knothole door to the Home Tree.

And there, in the Tree's pebbled courtyard, was Prilla, the new fairy, flat on her back, one wing bent, legs in the air, the remnants of the laugh collecting around her to form her Arrival Garment.

TWO

*M*OTHER DOVE knew the instant Prilla arrived. "The new fairy's come!" she told Beck excitedly. "Isn't that wonderful?"

"It is," Beck said, hoping the newcomer was an animal-talent fairy.

In the courtyard, a crowd gathered around Prilla. A message-talent fairy flew off to tell the queen.

Terence, a fairy-dust-talent sparrow man, sprinkled a level teacup of fairy dust on Prilla. Not a particle more than a cup nor a particle less, mind you. It was Prilla's first daily allotment.

As soon as the dust touched her, a tingly feeling spread over her, and her glow began. Fairies glow lemon-yellow, edged with gold.

She sat up. Her bent wing sprang back, and her wings started to flutter. Her mind cleared. She was a fairy! A Never fairy! She was so lucky!

The other fairies waited, feeling too solemn even to smile at the new arrival. Each fairy hoped against hope for a new talent member.

They expected her to announce her talent. The first act of every new fairy was to make The Announcement.

But Prilla flew over the courtyard, her brown hair streaming out behind her.

Flying was marvellous! She turned an aerial cartwheel.

And she had magical powers, didn't she? She flew to the Home Tree and shook a little fairy dust off her hand and onto a leaf. She squinted hard at the leaf, and it flickered out of sight. She blinked, and there it was again.

The fairies on the ground stared up at her. Not one of them had ever seen an arrival behave as Prilla was behaving. She landed in their midst, between Terence and a caterpillar herder.

They drew back.

"Greetings!" she said. "I'm so glad to be a fairy! Thank you for having me."

Several fairies raised their eyebrows. Did this newcomer think they'd picked her?

Prilla saw their expressions and faltered. "Er, I'll try to be a good fairy."

A fairy said, "My, she's freckled."

Terence said, "Pleasantly plump, though."

These were the sorts of things one said at an arrival, ordinarily after the new fairy had announced her talent.

"I swear they look younger every year," the caterpillar

herder said. A few fairies nodded.

Prilla wouldn't look young to you. She'd look grown-up, just about five inches tall, same as any other fairy, and perfectly proportioned. Fairies, however, knew that Prilla was a youngster, because her nose and the lower halves of her wings hadn't yet reached their full growth.

A grown-up Clumsy wouldn't see Prilla at all. He might see the air shimmer. He might smell cinnamon. He might hear leaves rustle, but he'd have no idea he was in the presence of a fairy.

Adult Clumsies can't see or hear fairies, although they can feel them. If a fairy pinches a grown-up Clumsy, the Clumsy will slap the spot, thinking he's been bitten by a mosquito.

Tinker Bell landed in the courtyard. When she'd seen Prilla flash by her workshop window, she had dropped her leaky ladle and come. She wanted to be on the spot if the new fairy turned out to have a talent for repairing pots and pans.

Terence smiled his most charming smile at Tink. He admired her enormously. He liked her bounce when she landed. He liked the arch of her eyebrows, the curl to her ponytail, and her bangs, which were the perfect length, whatever length they were. He even liked her scowl, which was both fierce and pert.

Tink ignored the smile. Her heart had been broken once, and she wasn't going to endanger it again. "Welcome to

Fairy Haven," she told Prilla. "What's your name, child?"

"Prilla." Prilla held out her hand to shake.

Tink hesitated, then shook. Fairies didn't usually shake hands. "I'm Tinker Bell."

Prilla said, "Pleased to meet you, Miss Bell."

The bystanders exchanged glances. Tink frowned.

Prilla blushed. She knew she'd said something wrong, but she had no idea what.

It was this: Never fairies called each other by their names. Just their names. No miss or mistering. And only Clumsies said Pleased to meet you. Never fairies said, I look forward to flying with you, or, for short, Fly with you.

"Call me Tink. What's your talent, Prilla?" Tink waited, barely breathing.

Prilla stopped seeing and hearing what was around her. Instead, she heard the strains of a waltz and Clumsy voices. She was back on the mainland, standing on the shoulder of a Clumsy girl who was riding a carousel horse.

The girl felt Prilla's wings beat against her neck and reached up to brush away what she thought was an insect. Prilla flew around to face the child, who turned slack-jawed with astonishment.

What fun! Prilla executed a perfect split and a double somersault.

Tink felt ignored. "Prilla, what's your talent?"

Prilla's grin faded. "Pardon me. What did you say?"

Tink tugged on her bangs. "Nobody says Pardon me. I said..." She spoke louder. "...what is your talent?"

"Talent?"

"Uh-oh," Terence said.

A wing washer said, "Is she a giggle shy of a full laugh?"

This happened sometimes. A piece of laugh would crack off on its way to the island, and the fairy would arrive incomplete. Some incompletes had no ear tips, or they'd glow on only half their bodies. Some looked complete, but they had a speech problem or they thought the word chicken rhymed with mattress.

In Prilla's case, the opposite was true. When Sara Quirtle laughed her first laugh, some of Sara stuck to it and went into Prilla. Prilla was fully a fairy, but she was more, as well.

"Par – er, excuse me, what's a talent?" Prilla asked.

The other fairies fluttered their wings, appalled.

"Nobody says Excuse me either," Tink said. "A talent is a special ability. All of us have one. We know what our talent is, from the moment we arrive."

Prilla couldn't think of a single thing she was good at. She blinked back tears. "I don't think I have a talent."

THREE

A BREEZE WHIPPED by Prilla's ears, and a fairy flew into the courtyard. She was Vidia, the fastest of the fast-flying-talent fairies. She landed before Prilla, and smiled.

Prilla didn't like that sugary smile.

Tink said, "Go away, Vidia."

Vidia said to Prilla, "Fly with you, dear child."

"P-pleased to meet you."

"Mmm. Incomplete, are we?" She leaned in close. "Dear child, if fast-flying is your talent, I have something that – "

"Vidia!" Tink said. She'd have to tell the queen about this. "You'd better – "

"Tink, darling ..."

Prilla thought the darling sounded like a sneer.

"...you have no idea – "

A sparrow man shot straight up into the air. "Hawk! Hawk from the west!"

Tink shoved Prilla through the knothole door to the Home Tree. The other fairies flew into the lower branches.

Prilla and Tink watched the shadow of a bird cross the courtyard.

"That was a hawk?" Prilla said.

Tink nodded.

"Would it have eaten us?"

"If it was hungry."

Hawks kill several fairies every year. Tink had had some close calls with them. She told Prilla, "Always keep a sharp eye out for hawks."

Prilla shuddered. "When it's safe, I'd like to thank that sparrow man. He saved us all."

Tink tugged her bangs, irritated. Something was wrong with Prilla, and when something was wrong, Tink wanted to fix it. That's why she loved repairing pots and pans. But she didn't know how to fix Prilla. It was like having an itch she couldn't reach. "Don't thank him. He's a scout."

Prilla looked blank.

Tink thought, I'm going to pull every hair out of my head. "Scouting is his talent. Saving us was his joy."

"I see," said Prilla. But she didn't.

Tink believed Prilla really had a talent but just didn't know what it was. She looked down at Prilla's hands. They were on the large side, but not too large. The child could be a pots-and-pans fairy. The strangest one ever.

Prilla was on the mainland again. She was on a breakfast table, next to a container of milk, eye-level with the words

Dietary fibre 0g on the container.

A man stood at the stove, pouring coffee. A boy was eating a muffin. Prilla flew in front of the boy's face, fascinated by his chewing.

"Look!" Crumbs and saliva shot out of his mouth. He lunged at Prilla. She retreated. He knocked over the milk.

She winked at him and was gone. Laughing, she told Tink, "I just saw a Clumsy spit out half a muffin."

Tink pulled her bangs. "What Clumsy?"

"The one…" Prilla realised she'd said something wrong again. Didn't Tink blink over to the mainland sometimes?

Of course Tink didn't. Most fairies had no contact with Clumsy children (other than the lost boys), unless a fellow fairy was dying of disbelief.

Prilla changed the subject. "Are we inside the Home Tree?"

"This is the lobby," Tink said, glad to talk about something reasonable.

The walls were golden brown, so highly buffed you could almost see your reflection.

Tink added proudly, "The walls are polished weekly, and it takes two dozen polishing-talent fairies to do it."

Prilla wondered if polishing might be her talent.

Next to the knothole door was a brass directory that listed each fairy, along with her talent, her room, and her workshop, if she had a workshop.

"Your name will be up there, too," Tink said, "in an hour or so, when the decor-talent fairies are through with your room."

Prilla nodded. She'd be the only one without a talent next to her name.

The lobby floor was tiled in pearly mica. A spiral staircase rose to the second story, although the fairies used it only when their wings were wet and they couldn't fly.

Four oval windows faced the courtyard.

"The windowpanes are reground pirate glass," Tink said. She thought longingly of her leaky ladle.

A clatter and a bang and raised voices came from the corridor beyond the lobby.

Prilla turned to Tink for an explanation.

Tink's heart raced. Something might have broken that she could fix. "Would you like to see the kitchen?"

"Can I?" Maybe she would have a talent for something there.

Tink had the same thought. Maybe she could leave Prilla in the kitchen and get back to her workshop. Or, if a pot really had broken, Tink could find out right there if Prilla had any talent for fixing it.

"Come," Tink said.

Prilla followed her into the corridor, which was lined with paintings of the symbols for each talent – a feather for the fairy-dust talent, a dented stew pot for the pots-and-pans talent, the sun for the light talent. Prilla wondered what the painting of a nose and half a moustache stood for.

Tink patted the gilded frame of the stew-pot painting as she flew by. Then she turned in to the first doorway they came to. Prilla followed and smelled nutmeg. Her stomach rumbled. It had never done that before, and she wondered what it meant.

"This is the tearoom," Tink said. "It's Queen Ree's favourite room." Ree was the fairies' nickname for Queen Clarion. "You'll meet Ree at the celebration tonight."

Meet the queen! Prilla's glow flared. The queen!

Prilla studied the tearoom, looking for clues to Queen Ree in her favourite room. The mood was serene, the colours muted. The narrow windows stretched from a few inches above the floral carpet to the lofty ceiling, fifteen inches away. The daylight, filtered through maple leaves outside and Queen-Anne's-lace curtains inside, was the same green as the Never pale-grass wallpaper.

Tink added, "It's nice, but I like more metal in a room."

Most everyone took their tea later in the day. Now, only a few fairies sipped from the periwinkle teacups or ate crustless sandwiches on cockleshell plates. They watched Prilla with interest.

Prilla thought, I could take the crusts off the sandwich bread. I wouldn't need much talent to have a talent for that.

Tink led her past a serving table holding a platter of star-shaped butter cookies, each point perfect and not a single one broken. Prilla would have liked to stop for a cookie, but Tink was hurrying ahead, so she decided she'd better not.

Tink pointed to an empty table under a silver chandelier. "I sit there with the rest of my talent."

"The talents sit together?"

Tink nodded.

"So who..." Prilla trailed off. She'd been about to ask who sat with you if you didn't have a talent. But she knew the answer. Nobody. You sat alone.

FOUR

*T*INK PUSHED open the swinging door to the kitchen.
Prilla's wings skipped a beat. She had never seen so
many fairies.

Fairies from twenty-five talents were at work in the
kitchen. Some of the talents were quite specialised – sub-
talents, really – such as the knowing-when-a-dish-is-done
talent or the stove-to-plate-transfer talent.

The air was full of flying fairies. But as soon as Prilla
entered, they all froze, registering her presence.

Prilla blushed so deeply that her glow turned orange.

Everyone went back to work. Tink looked for the source of
the clatter she and Prilla had heard in the lobby. There it
was, shattered china and a pool of pea soup – nothing to
interest a pots-and-pans fairy.

Then Tink's eyes were drawn to the racks that rose to the
ceiling. She saw the steamer she'd fixed last week. And there
was the pressure cooker that had given her endless trouble,
and the circular tube pan that had kept going oblong.

She knew it was silly, but she couldn't resist a little wave
to each of them.

She turned to Prilla. If the child had any kitchen kind of talent, it would show on her face. She'd be all smiles, excited, eager.

But Prilla's expression was vague, her eyes glassy. Tink had seen her wear that expression before.

Prilla was on the windowsill of a Clumsy girl's bedroom. On the floor was an assortment of doll furniture. A large doll overwhelmed a chair at a kitchen table. A small doll stood nearby, its head barely clearing the top of the table.

The Clumsy girl was searching for something in a brown paper bag.

Prilla flew to the toy stove and put one hand on the handle of a kettle. She folded her wings, made herself doll-still, and tried to lower her glow. Inside she was roaring with laughter. Would the Clumsy think her a new doll?

The girl turned back. "I wish I ... Wha – "

"Prilla!"

Prilla jumped in the air. There was Tink, one hand on her bangs and the other on her hip.

"What were you ... Never mind." Tink didn't care what Prilla had been doing. "You don't see anything you're talented at, do you?"

"I don't know. Maybe."

Tink sighed. "You'd know."

Prilla sighed, too. She wondered if she could get away with pretending to have a talent.

Dulcie, a baking-talent fairy, flew to them bearing a basket of poppy puff rolls. "Try one."

Prilla and Tink helped themselves. It was Prilla's first food ever, and she wasn't sure what to expect. She felt her mouth water, which was curious. She bit in cautiously.

Dulcie said, "Are you the new fairy? Fly with you. Is the roll too salty?"

Prilla was too busy tasting to answer. She shut her eyes. The roll wasn't too salty. It was perfect, except that it melted away too fast. She took another bite. Mmm. Buttery. A little poppy-seed crunch. A hint of sweetness. A hint of a herb. Tarragon. She loved it. She'd like about ten more rolls. Eating was a joy.

Joy! Prilla remembered what Tink had said about the scout. Scouting was his joy.

She opened her eyes. "I have a talent!" She turned a cartwheel. "Tink, I have a talent. My talent is eating."

Tink reached for her bangs. "That's not a talent. Everyone loves Dulcie's rolls."

"Oh." Why isn't it a talent, Prilla wondered, even if everybody else also has it?

Dulcie said to Tink, "It's true then? She doesn't know what her talent is?"

Prilla felt herself blush again. She wished she were still a laugh.

FIVE

A cry came from the other side of the kitchen. "Tink! Is that you? Come here!"

Tink flew off. Prilla started after her and collided with a fairy carrying a sack of hayseed flour. Both of them wound up covered with flour.

"I'm sorry," Prilla said.

The fairy said, "Nobody says sorry," and flew away.

Prilla dusted herself off while wondering what they did say. She began to fly after Tink but stopped mid-flutter. Tink was being embraced by a fairy who was standing in a coconut-shell tub and weeping.

The weeping fairy was Rani, the most ardent of the water-talent fairies.

Improbably, the two were fast friends. Three years before, Rani had brought Tink an egg poacher to fix. She had praised Tink's repair so enthusiastically that Tink had been won over.

"The coating cracked!" Rani wailed.

Prilla came close and hovered behind Tink.

"What – " Tink began.

" – cracked?" Rani said, finishing the question she thought Tink was asking.

Tink shook her head. " – did you do to your wings?"

Prilla stared. Rani's wings were covered with what looked like dried and flaking mucus.

"It's just egg, for waterproofing." Rani blew her nose on a leafkerchief. "Now my wings have to be washed, and I won't be able to fly tonight."

Rani wanted desperately to swim. Never fairies can't, you know. Their wings absorb water and drag them under.

She had persuaded a baking-talent fairy to coat her wings with beaten egg. She'd hoped the egg would make them waterproof. So, when the egg had dried, she'd climbed into the tub and lowered her wings into the water. At first, all was well. But as soon as she'd moved a wing, its coating had cracked.

Tink began, "At least you didn't use a – "

" – balloon." Rani started laughing so hard she was weeping again. Because of her talent, Rani cried easily, sweated easily, and her nose tended to run. As she herself put it, she was as full of water as a watermelon.

She said, "I'll never try to swim with a balloon again."

Tink said, "Maybe not a balloon ..." She smiled.

Prilla hadn't seen Tink smile before. Tink had dimples! And when she smiled, she looked like someone you didn't have to be afraid of talking to.

Tink went on. "But you'll try something – "

" – else." Rani smiled back. "Probably." She noticed Prilla. "You're the new fairy! Just in time for the celebration!" She wondered why the child wasn't with her whole talent, trying things out. And why did she look sad? "I'm Rani. Fly with you. Everyone is so glad you've come."

Prilla thought, Nobody seems glad. "Fly with you. I'm Prilla." She braced herself for the talent question.

Rani stepped out of the tub. "I have the worst talent, Prilla. It's breaking my heart. I hope you're not a water-talent fairy."

Prilla shrugged. She wished she were.

Rani looked questioningly at Tink.

Tink's smile vanished. "She doesn't know what her talent – "

" – is. Really?" Rani thought, Oh, the poor child. She said, "Lucky you. You can try them all out."

Prilla felt like the least lucky fairy in Neverland. What if she tried them all and had none?

"Let's see if you have a water talent," Rani said. "Come closer to the tub."

Prilla landed and approached the tub. If only, she thought. If only I could be a water-talent fairy.

"Watch." Rani brushed a grain or two of fairy dust from her wrist into the water. Then she reached into the tub and scooped up a handful of water.

Prilla's eyes widened. The water didn't run through Rani's

fingers. Instead, it stayed in her hand, a ball of water.

With her free hand, Rani pinched the water here and pulled it there until it took the shape of a fish with a gaping mouth. She passed her hand over it, and its scales gleamed gold and its eyes turned iridescent.

Prilla drew in a breath. Tink's smile returned.

Rani said, "That takes practise. This too." She balled up the water again and tilted her hand. The ball dropped into the tub, but stayed a ball. She raised her hand a little, and the ball rose to meet it. In a moment she was bouncing the water ball into the tub and out again.

Prilla wanted to shout her delight or turn a somersault.

Rani threw the ball into the air and caught it. Again. Again. Then she missed. The water ball landed on the floor, rolled an inch, and stopped near Prilla's feet.

Prilla drew back a step.

"Try picking it up," Rani said. "If you have a talent for water, you'll be able to."

Prilla's hands trembled. Please let me be a water-talent fairy, she thought.

She bent over and reached for the water ball.

SIX

*T*HE WATER ball dissolved into a puddle the instant Prilla touched it.

She looked up at Rani, her eyes full of tears. Rani drew the puddle up and dumped it into the tub without leaving a drop on the floor. She was crying too. Tink was more irritated than ever. Now two fairies needed fixing.

But Rani brightened. "Tink, did you take Prilla to meet Mother Dove?"

"No."

Prilla knew who Mother Dove was. Knowing was part of being a Never fairy.

"Oh, Tink. She'll know what Prilla's talent is."

Mother Dove understood fairies better than fairies understood themselves.

"Prilla," Rani added, her face shining, "I can't wait for you to meet Mother Dove."

Tink said, "We'll go now."

Prilla saw that Tink was smiling again, looking unTinkishly happy.

Tink and Prilla flew out the tree-bark-side kitchen door.

Outside, the wind was sharp. They didn't know it, but the wind was coming from a hurricane that was chasing Neverland up and down the ocean.

As she flew, Prilla worried that Mother Dove wouldn't love her. She was the first fairy not to know what her talent was, maybe the first not to have a talent. What if she was the first fairy Mother Dove didn't love? What if she was the first fairy Mother Dove hated?

Prilla flew toward a Clumsy boy who was burying his teddy bear in his mainland backyard. She tweaked the boy's ear and flew on after Tink.

Tink felt proud to be bringing Prilla to Mother Dove. The wanded fairies had their wands. The spell fairies had their spells, and the shimmerers had their shimmers. But the Never fairies had Mother Dove, and Tink wouldn't have changed places with the others for anything.

After half an hour of flying against the wind, Tink and Prilla finally reached Mother Dove's hawthorn tree.

Tink stopped and hovered a few feet above the nest to let Prilla see Mother Dove before meeting her. This was uncommonly kind of Tink. If both events had happened at once, Prilla would have been too excited to form a clear memory. She wouldn't have been able to think, in the time to come, *This was when I saw her; this was when our eyes met;*

this was when she spoke.

Mother Dove cooperated. She was aware of Tink and Prilla, but she didn't look up. Give the child a chance to collect herself, she thought.

And how was it for Prilla or any fairy to see Mother Dove for the first time?

Picture a cottage. Your cottage might have a thatched roof. Mine might have a blue door with a brass knocker. The walls of yours might be a soft grey with pink trim. Daisies might bloom by the open door. A golden light might twinkle out.

You see the cottage and recognise that it's exactly what you've always wanted, although a moment earlier you had no idea.

That's how Mother Dove was for fairies. More than the Home Tree, more than Fairy Haven, she was their home.

Prilla sighed, completely satisfied.

Tink started down to the nest. Prilla followed. Please love me, she thought. Mother Dove, please love me. Please know what my talent is. Please. Please.

Tink landed on the edge of the nest, but Prilla was afraid to come so close. She hovered almost a foot away.

Mother Dove smiled at Prilla. Mother Dove's eyes smiled too, and her neck feathers stood out with pleasure. She cooed a string of coos, happy musical gurgles. She saw how sweet and merry and smart and acrobatic Prilla was.

Prilla smiled blissfully at Mother Dove.

Beck, the animal-talent fairy who took care of Mother Dove, smiled too. She loved to see Mother Dove's effect on new fairies.

"You're Prilla, aren't you?" Mother Dove said. "Prilla." She peeped the p and rolled the r and ls. "You've come where you belong, Prilla. I'm glad as can be that you're here."

SEVEN

*T*HANK YOU." Prilla felt so relieved. Mother Dove did love her. Prilla wanted to throw herself into Mother Dove's fluffy feathers and stay there, safe.

Mother Dove sensed Prilla's blinks over to the mainland and her blank spots about being a fairy. "You've had a hard arrival, haven't you?"

Prilla nodded, feeling understood for the first time.

Mother Dove cocked her head. She couldn't see the future in any detail, but she sometimes saw hints. "I'm afraid your hard arrival isn't over yet. You'll need your inner resources."

Prilla nodded again. With Mother Dove looking at her so sympathetically, Prilla felt she had inner resources for anything. She turned a cartwheel in the air. "I don't mind."

Pleased, Mother Dove said, "Would you like to see my egg?"

Beck was surprised. Mother Dove didn't show her egg to every new arrival.

"May I?"

Mother Dove raised herself on one leg. "I never get off completely."

Prilla saw a pale blue egg, bigger than an ordinary dove's egg and smoother than the finest pearl.

"It's very pretty," Prilla said politely. She didn't see anything extraordinary about it.

But it was extraordinary. It was this egg that kept all the animals and Clumsies on the island from growing old. The egg was responsible for the *Never* in Neverland.

"Thank you." Mother Dove cooed happily. "Do you know, Beck, I think Prilla is hungry." Mother Dove loved it when a new fairy was hungry. "Is anything left of the nutmeg pie?"

Beck opened her picnic basket and cut a slice of pie. She lifted the slice onto a plate and placed the plate on the nest in front of Mother Dove.

Mother Dove pecked off a fairy-size bite and held it out in her beak.

Prilla took it. Ah. It was as good as Dulcie's roll.

Mother Dove pecked off another bite, and Prilla took it. Of course Beck could have given Prilla a fork, and Prilla could have eaten on her own. But this was better. The nutmeg pie was sweet. Mother Dove's love was sweeter.

Bite by bite, Mother Dove fed Prilla the rest of the pie.

Tink closed her eyes, remembering Mother Dove's first words to her. *Oh, my,* Mother Dove had said. *You're Tinker Bell, sound and fine as a bell. Shiny and jaunty as a new pot.*

Brave enough for anything, the most courageous fairy to come in a long year. Then Mother Dove had fed her. Tink had known, and still knew, that Mother Dove loved her, from her toes to her ponytail.

Finally, the last crumb of pie was gone. Prilla reeled back, dizzy with fullness and feeling.

Tink came out of her reverie. "Mother Dove, do you know what Prilla's talent is? She doesn't." Tink paused, feeling uncomfortable, then blurted out, "Is she incomplete?"

Prilla was astounded. Tink thought her incomplete?

"There's nothing wrong with being incomplete," Mother Dove said, a hint of sharpness in her tone.

"Am I incomplete?" Prilla asked, scared.

"Prilla is complete."

Prilla thought, What's my talent? Say it, Mother Dove. Say it.

Mother Dove cocked her head again. She became aware of something new about Prilla, something that had never before been in Neverland. "You have a talent dear, but I don't know what it is."

"Will I find it?"

Mother Dove smiled. "I believe you will."

Believe? Prilla thought. She just believes? What if she's wrong?

GAIL CARSON LEVINE

"Could Prilla be an animal talent?" Beck said. "We need help with the chipmunks." She turned to Prilla. "Do you like chipmunks? They're big and sometimes dangerous, but they're honourable."

Prilla nodded. She didn't know if she liked chipmunks, but she was desperate for a talent. And if she were an animal-talent fairy, perhaps she could be Mother Dove's companion when Beck was busy.

"She isn't an animal talent, Beck," Mother Dove said. "She doesn't knock on the door of my thoughts, as a beginner would, or slip right in, as you do."

Prilla tried to knock on Mother Dove's thoughts. But nothing happened.

"Each talent is glorious, Prilla," Mother Dove said. "When you find yours, you'll be part of its glory. Would you like to see what Beck can do?"

"Yes, please." Prilla was curious, although she expected to be awfully jealous.

Tink burst out, "I have a ladle to fix!" She hadn't wasted this much time since her days with Peter.

Mother Dove nodded agreeably. "Yes, dear."

Tink knew what that meant. It meant, *Hush, Tink.* It meant, *Your ladle can wait.*

Beck shook a grain or two of fairy dust on a swarm of

midges flying below the nest. She beckoned, and a midge flew to her.

Beck held out her finger, and the midge landed on it.

Prilla shrank back. Ugh!

Beck said, "Midges love this. Watch. Bump. Ump." At bump the midge flew straight up. On ump it came down to Beck's finger. "Bump, ump." Up, down. "Bump ump, bump ump." Up, down, up down. Beck spoke faster. The midge upped and downed faster.

Prilla found herself nodding in time with the midge. Tink kept thinking about her ladle. Mother Dove noticed the wind again. She'd been noticing it on and off all day.

Beck spoke faster and faster. The midge became a frenzied blur. Beck's words began to run together, and the midge stopped.

"Thank you," Beck said, laughing. She flicked her finger at Prilla.

The midge flew to Prilla and landed on her nose. A midge on a fairy was as big as a bee on a Clumsy. Prilla stiffened. She crossed her eyes, trying to watch it, wishing it would go away but afraid to brush it off. It climbed up her nose and then back down, exploring with its antennae.

"Thank you," Beck said again. "We're finished."

The midge flew away. Prilla relaxed, and realised she

wasn't jealous of Beck. Not a smidgen. She smiled inwardly. Not a s-midge-n.

"Now you can go to your ladle, Tink," Mother Dove said. "Show Prilla your workshop."

"Do you want to see it?" Tink would have liked to be rid of Prilla – except for the chance she might be a pots-and-pans fairy.

Prilla nodded, although she would rather have stayed with Mother Dove.

"Prilla could be a tinker," Mother Dove said. "It's possible."

Tink's wingtips quivered. "Come, Prilla."

The wind was worse on the way back to the Home Tree. When they got there, Tink flew to the second story and pulled open a door under a steel awning.

"This is it." She always felt shy when someone saw the workshop for the first time.

But Prilla wasn't seeing it. She was in a mainland toy shop, lying on a railway track. Yeow! A locomotive was streaking toward her, smoke billowing. She flew straight up and then raced the train, laughing as she flew.

"Look!" a Clumsy girl yelled. "A little fairy!"

Prilla turned and flew backward, waving at the girl, half concealed by smoke.

"Watch out!" Tink yelled.

EIGHT

*P*RILLA FLEW into a hanging basket. The basket rocked, spewing rivets.

Tink was on the floor, picking up rivets, too angry to scold. She thought Prilla was as clumsy as a Clumsy.

"Sorry!"

"Nobody says *sorry*."

Prilla picked up rivets, too. The parquet floor was painted white, so they were easy to see. She peeked at the room around her.

Oh! She sat back on her haunches, rivets forgotten. Oh! The workshop walls and ceiling were shiny steel. The room was circular, and the ceiling was domed.

Prilla wondered, Am I? Could it be?

Tink smiled at her astonishment.

Prilla saw Tink's smile and found the courage to ask, "Am I inside a big... pot?"

Tink's dimples came out again. "It was a Clumsy's teakettle. I found it on the beach."

Tink had hammered out its dents and had cleaned and polished it inside and out. Then, with the power of a gallon of fairy dust and with Mother Dove's advice on the magic, Tink had squeezed the kettle into the Home Tree and expanded it again. She'd turned the spout upside down to make the door awning, and she'd punched out openings for windows and doors.

"We're inside a teakettle?" Prilla spun around. "A teakettle! Oh, my! You're so talented, Tink." Talented. Now she was saying it.

"Thank you." Tink couldn't help adding, "It's the only inside-a-pot workshop on the island."

Prilla said, "Could I see something you've fixed?"

Tink flew to a table by the door, where she kept jobs that hadn't yet been picked up. She raised an iron frying pan, using a bit of levitation to lighten it. "I finished this one yesterday. A piece had broken off."

"I see it," Prilla said, following a jagged outline with her finger. She didn't think Tink could be very accomplished if her repair stood out so clearly.

Tink started to laugh. "That's a ..." She was laughing too hard to finish the sentence. "It's a ..." A minute passed. Tink kept laughing.

Prilla didn't see anything the slightest bit funny.

Finally, Tink's laughter died down. "It's a joke. That's not where it broke. I just put that there ..." Her laughter bubbled up again. "... to fool everyone."

Prilla smiled uneasily.

Tink sobered. "Try to find the real place where it broke." It was as good a test as any. If Prilla found it, she was in.

Prilla's glow vibrated with nervousness. She took the frying pan and inspected it. "Umm ..." She brought the pan almost to her nose. She didn't see anything. Except for the false crack, the frying pan was utterly smooth, utterly black. She turned it over.

On the back of the handle was Tink's talent mark, a drawing in red enamel paint of a tiny pot with squiggly lines for steam rising from it. Across the pot were the letters *TB*.

Prilla saw the mark, but nothing else. She knew she'd failed. Tink hadn't liked her much before, but she'd like her even less now. "I can't find it."

Tink was surprised at how let down she felt. Now Prilla still needed fixing, and the pots and pans didn't have a new fairy, and the ladle was still leaky.

"This is the real break," Tink said. She traced a crack that Prilla still couldn't see. "Come, I'll show you what I'm working on now."

Prilla forced a smile.

Tink went to the pots and pans on her worktable, her wonderful pile, days and days of puzzles for her to solve. She took the leaky ladle from the top of the pile and held it up. "This is it."

The ladle was made of Never pewter, a smoky blue variety

produced only on Neverland. "It doesn't always leak, but when it does, it leaks mulberry juice, only mulberry juice, no matter what liquid it's dipped in. It's a fascinating case."

The ladle would be needed often tonight, and if it wasn't fixed, the leak was sure to show up.

"I don't know," Tink went on, "where the leak is or if it's a pinprick leak or a squiggle leak." She sat on a stool at the worktable and cupped her hand around the bowl of the ladle. Her glow in that hand intensified. She crooned, "Are you an instant or a gradual leak?"

She forgot Prilla completely. She wasn't trying to be unkind. But she wasn't trying to be kind, either.

Prilla hovered quietly, feeling lonelier than ever.

Ten minutes passed. Tink selected jars and tubes of different sorts of adhesive. She mixed a little of this and a little of that in a bowl.

Prilla edged toward the door. Why did she have to stay here? Her talent – if she had one – was elsewhere. She should be looking for it.

She reached the door and glanced back. Tink's head was down, over the ladle.

Prilla said, too softly for Tink to hear, "I'm leaving now. Thank you for showing me your workshop. Good-bye." She pushed the door open and slipped out.

NINE

Outside, Prilla found dozens of fairies, standing on branches or hovering, waiting for her. Word had travelled that the new fairy didn't know what her talent was.

Someone called out, "Do you think you'd like shearing caterpillars?" Someone else said, "Isn't it fun to dry toadstools?"

Prilla recognised Terence, the dust fairy, near the front of the crowd, and she thought another fairy looked familiar, too, maybe from the tearoom or the kitchen.

A fairy cried, "Don't you love washing wings?" And another, "How about weaving grass?"

They all began shouting at once.

"Sorting sand?"

"Cricket whistling?"

"Grading tree bark?"

Prilla flattened herself against Tink's door, frightened.

Then she was in a Clumsy supermarket, wedged in with a bunch of broccoli, a rubber band tight around her waist. A Clumsy boy bounded toward her.

The boy called over his shoulder, "Mom, can we get broccoli?"

The woman hurried over. "Broccoli? Absolutely!" She reached for the bunch next to Prilla.

"No, I want that bunch."

Laughing, Prilla said, "Don't cook me!"

A fairy jostled her. Prilla flinched.

"Me first!" someone called out.

"No, me!"

"Stop pushing!" Terence said, his voice deep and resonant. "We're frightening her." He smiled at Prilla, the same winsome smile that Tink had failed to see. "I'm Terence...."

A voice in the crowd rang out, "Why should you go first?"

Prilla thought, Terence glitters.

"Because," Terence said, "if Prilla's a dust fairy, she has to get ready for the Molt."

That convinced them. The Molt was urgent.

Terence did glitter. It was the fairy dust that clung to his oak- leaf frock coat and caught his glow light.

"Prilla, would you like to visit the mill and see if you're a dust fairy?"

Prilla nodded, although she thought it was probably too much to hope for.

They flew off. Terence shouted over the wind, "Did Tinker Bell mention me to you?"

"No," Prilla shouted back.

"Oh. I see."

Prilla heard the disappointment in his voice. He likes Tink! she thought. She shouted, "Tink didn't mention anyone."

"Ah."

They flew on without any more conversation. Prilla wondered what dust fairies did. If they only poured a cup of dust over everybody every day, she could do that. She wouldn't mind waking up early.

Terence began to descend. Soon they landed on the bank of Havendish Stream.

"The mill is around the next bend," Terence said. "But first...do you know what dust does?"

Prilla had known as soon as she became a fairy. "Dust helps us fly. Without dust, we can fly a foot or so; but with it, we can fly any distance. Dust makes everything go. It powers the mill. It goes in the balloons for the balloon carriers. We can barely glow without it." She smiled, feeling like a star pupil.

"Do you know where dust comes from?"

Prilla thought a moment. "From Mother Dove! After she molts we grind up her feathers. Dust is ground feathers." Oh, Prilla thought, understanding. "That's why we're celebrating tonight. Mother Dove is about to molt. She molts every year, right?"

"Right. What do we do?"

"We?"

"Dust fairies."

Prilla's glow flared. Was Terence suggesting she might be one of them? One of *we*. "They – we – give out dust to every fairy every day."

"What else?"

She thought hard, anxious to hold on to the we. "Um, we set aside a portion for Peter Pan and the lost boys." There was probably more to it. "Um, we collect the feathers after the Molt and grind them." Prilla pictured Mother Dove. "We sort the feathers into wings, back, neck, belly. Do we grind them in the mill in certain proportions?"

Terence nodded, beginning to feel hope. "What else?"

Prilla was thinking like mad. "We make sure nothing blows away, not the smallest grain. We make sure the dust doesn't get wet. We store the dust in...in something big." Prilla's wings drooped. "I don't know what we store it in."

But Terence was smiling. "Very good." He thought she'd done well, better than a new fairy in another talent would have. "We store it in dried-pumpkin canisters. Come, I'll take you to the mill." He started flying.

Prilla did a handstand and sprang into the air after him.

But he came down again. "Watch out for Vidia," he said.

She landed next to him. "Vidia?"

"Vidia! You met her outside the Home Tree when you arrived. She calls everyone *darling* and *sweetheart*."

Prilla nodded, remembering. "She sneered at Tink. Why do we watch out for her?"

"She's stolen dust more than once. She hurt Mother Dove, too." Terence didn't like speaking ill of anyone, but in Vidia's case, he had a responsibility. "Vidia plucked living feathers from Mother Dove, and plucking hurts."

"Why did she do that?" Prilla asked, shocked.

"To fly faster. Feathers that are fresh, that don't come from the Molt, are supposed to make you fly faster. Vidia's talent is fast flying, you know."

Prilla resolved that she'd never hurt anyone for the sake of her talent – if she turned out to have a talent.

Terence added, "She got ten feathers before a scout caught her. Queen Ree has banned her from Mother Dove's presence." He flapped his wings, glad to be done with the subject of Vidia. "Ready for the mill?"

Prilla followed him into the air, but he came down again, and so did she.

"I have a saucepan," he said. "I could dent it and bring it to Tink to fix. Do you think..." He trailed off.

"Don't just dent it," Prilla said. "Squash it or put a hole in it. The worse it is, the better she'll like it."

"Ah," Terence said. "I'll take your advice." He jumped into the air, and this time he kept going.

The mill, which was built of peach pits and mortar, spanned Havendish Stream. As he unlatched the big double doors, Terence said, "If you're one of us, you'll be spending a lot of your time here."

The wind pushed the doors open.

He added, "The tree-pickers use the mill, too. But not today, because of the celebration."

The mill was empty and quiet. Daylight streamed in through the small windows just below the roof. Prilla saw the mill works – the grindstones, the wheel, the hopper – and across from them a dozen pumpkin canisters.

She wasn't feeling the joy other fairies felt from their talents, but she thought that might be because she hadn't yet done anything with dust. She pointed at the grindstones. "You could squash your saucepan in there."

"In there?" Terence was horrified. "Where Mother Dove's feathers go?"

She'd said something wrong again. "I was just joking."

"Oh." Terence didn't think a saucepan in the mill was funny. He perched on the top of an open pumpkin canister. "Look, Prilla. This is all the dust we have left." He flew into the canister.

Prilla followed. The dust was only three inches deep. It sparkled faintly.

"It looks so...so...so..." She sneezed. And sneezed five more rapid-fire sneezes.

Luckily, she was too high up to blow any dust away, but still Terence frowned.

She knew why he was frowning. You couldn't be a dust-talent fairy if three inches of dust made you sneeze.

TEN

*O*n the way back to the Home Tree, Prilla hugged her Arrival Garment close to keep it from being dragged open by the wind. Her disappointment over the dust stayed with her, a lump in her throat that had grown with each talent failure.

Terence left her in the lobby, after telling her that everyone would gather for the celebration in about an hour. He added, "Tonight is our busiest night. Once the Molt starts, we can't stop. It's marvellous."

Prilla smiled weakly, and Terence flew outside.

She didn't know what to do next. She could go to Tink, but Tink wouldn't want her. She would have liked to find Rani, the water-talent fairy, but she didn't know where to look. She wanted to leave the lobby before someone came along, asking her to try out another talent she wouldn't have.

She wondered if she had a room yet. She looked herself up on the directory, and there she was!

Prilla ·················Room 7P, NNW Branch

The dots in the middle were where her talent listing should have been.

She flew up the spiral staircase. After the first floor, there were no more stairs. There were just holes in the ceiling, and ladders for fairies to climb if their wings were wet. On the seventh floor she followed signs through the northwest trunk quadrant and took the right fork for the north-northwest branch.

By the time she reached her door, the corridor wasn't much taller than she was. Her room wasn't one of the better ones. Her tree-bark–side door was partially blocked by a cluster of leaves, and her window looked out on a twig.

Decorating the room had posed a problem for the decor-talent fairies. The theme of every other fairy bedroom was the occupant's talent.

In Tink's room, the bed frame was a pirate's loaf pan. Her three lamps had colander lampshades. And the painting over the bed was a still life of a stockpot, a whisk, and a griddle. In Rani's room, the ceiling had a permanent leak, which dripped into a thimble tub where a Never minnow swam. In Terence's room, there were lots of knick knacks, so the room was always dusty.

But the decor fairies hadn't known what to do for Prilla. As a result, they gave her plain, ordinary everything. Her bedposts were ho-hum reinforced daisy stems. The canopy was a fanned cabbage leaf in the same pale sea foam that everyone but the textile talents got. The lacy bedspread was boring triple-ply spiderweb. The night table was toadstool with snail-shell inlay in a geometric pattern. And so on – a profusion of commonplace fairy furnishings.

Prilla didn't see any of it. What she did see were the dresses and ensembles laid out on the bed, and the footwear spread out below.

She started toward the bed just as the wind outside made the Home Tree sway. She stumbled back against her door.

The gust passed. She went to the bed and picked up one thing after another. She rubbed fabrics against her cheek and held dresses up against herself. At least some fairy cared enough about her to make such beautiful things.

She tried on the violet wrap dress first. It had short sleeves, three pearl buttons, and a scalloped hemline.

Prilla was on the floor of a Clumsy girl's bedroom. The girl was attempting to dress her in a similar wrap dress, only this one was paisley, and the hem was frilly, not scalloped.

The girl couldn't get Prilla's wings into the dress's wing slits. "Hold still," she said, lifting Prilla and holding her by one wing.

It didn't hurt. Never fairy wings don't feel pain. Prilla didn't move a muscle.

The girl couldn't push the wings through.

"The wing slits are too short," Prilla said.

"No, they're not."

Prilla grinned. "Are too."

"Are not!"

"Are too!"

"Are not!" The girl let go of Prilla, and she fell to the floor, her wings tangled up in the dress.

The real wrap dress fit perfectly, the wing slits exactly the right length. And when Prilla whirled, the scalloped skirt fluttered deliciously against her bare legs.

Next, she put on a gold dress and had trouble tying the wide sash in the back. She wished she had a friend. A friend could tie your sash for you.

The friend could be her same size and could try on the dresses, too, like the blue tulip with the tight skirt that flared at the knees.

Prilla put on a pair of baggy trousers and a loose-fitting scoop-necked pullover, both made of felt as soft as mist. She wondered what the other fairies would be wearing. Was the celebration a dressy affair?

A friend who knew the ropes could tell her.

Well, she didn't have a friend, and that was that. She crouched to examine the shoes and slippers and boots.

Fairy footwear is nowhere near as sturdy as Clumsy footwear.

The heels on a pair of dressy shoes were as thin as needles. A pair of sandals had toe-weaving, and there were boots with spaghetti laces. The bedroom slippers were mouse-shaped, with a long blue tail.

The shoes fit as perfectly as everything else. Prilla wondered how they'd done it, then guessing it was talent again. Probably a measuring-talent fairy had seen her for a split second and had divined the circumference of her elbows, the length of her kneecaps, and the precise distance from her ankle to her big toe.

She sighed and considered what to wear. She decided she'd better dress up, and chose the green-and-white dotted organdy with puffed sleeves and tiny pleats. Looking in the mirror, she was pretty sure the dots went well with her freckles, but she wished a friend were there to say she was right.

For shoes she chose the white open-toes with the roll-back heels.

She brushed her hair and pinned up one side with the abalone-shell barrette she found in the top dressing-table drawer. Then she looked in the full-length mirror.

I look nice, she thought, and burst into tears.

If only she had a friend.

If only she had a talent.

Then she'd have a friend.

ELEVEN

*P*RILLA THREW herself on the bed, sobbing. She felt sure there would be no place for her at the celebration. The only one who wanted her was Mother Dove, who was probably busy celebrating and getting ready to molt. Prilla cried so hard she didn't notice the Home Tree swaying in the wind again.

She wept until she fell asleep.

But not simply asleep.

She was perched atop the head of a Clumsy girl who was following a path through a forest. A light glinted ahead. Soon they reached a farmhouse. The farmhouse door opened, and three cornstalks hopped out.

Prilla didn't find out what happened next because –

She was falling out of a skyscraper with a different Clumsy girl. The ground was coming close when Prilla shook some fairy dust on the girl. They both began to fly.

She was in a rainstorm with half a dozen green-skinned Clumsy children who were jumping like frogs from one puddle to another.

She was passing from one Clumsy child's dream to another. The scenes changed more and more quickly. A platter of meatballs, each with an eyeball peering out. A whale with elephant tusks, a Clumsy baby with a curly red beard, a mountain, a castle, a sea of silver spoons.

At the fairy circle, the celebration was getting under way. Night had fallen. Lanterns were flaring and guttering in the rising wind, but fairy glow made everything festive.

The cooking talents were still unpacking, but the serving-talent fairies were already passing around barley crackers topped with mouse Brie. The servers had to back into the wind to protect their offerings.

Bess, the renowned painter, had brought her new portrait of Mother Dove, which was to be unveiled later on. Terence and the other dust fairies were weighing down their Molt sacks with stones to keep them from blowing away. The light-talent fairies were preparing for their show, which was always the first event, even before Queen Ree's speech.

Vidia was lurking in the upper branches of the hawthorn. She'd been banned from the celebration, but she intended to fly in the fast-flier race anyway. No one would be able to stop her once the race began.

She'd brought along a few grains of dust from the feathers

she'd plucked, *fresh* dust, as she called it. When she'd done the plucking, Vidia hadn't enjoyed hurting Mother Dove. She'd cringed every time Mother Dove had groaned. But she'd persuaded herself that Mother Dove was exaggerating the pain. Since each plucking lasted only a second, Vidia had decided it couldn't be so terrible.

And now, the fresh dust would guarantee her victory in the race.

Beck tightened the bow on Mother Dove's ribbon, bracing herself against Mother Dove's chest. "How is your tingle?"

"Coming along." The pre-Molt tingle would gain strength during the night, until the celebration would fade and there would be only tingle. Then feathers would begin to drop off. The tingle would stop, and there would be blessed peace.

"Can I do anything?" Beck always asked, although she knew there was nothing to do.

"No, thank you. Where do you think Prilla is?" It would be a shame if the child missed her first celebration.

Beck didn't know, and Moth, the most talented of the light talents, came over to say they were ready to begin.

Everyone settled on branches or on the ground around Mother Dove's nest. They lowered their glows.

Moth positioned herself a foot from Mother Dove's head. The other light fairies took their places closer to Mother

Dove, surrounding her. They brightened their glows, brighter, brighter, as bright as they could make them.

It was Moth's turn.

She squinted and clenched her teeth. She made the glows around Mother Dove's tail flare even brighter, ten times brighter, twenty times brighter.

The watching fairies sighed. *Ah.*

Moth moved the extra brightness from Mother Dove's tail to Mother Dove's head, and then onto her wings, her belly, and back to her tail. It was hard to keep up the extra brilliance, hard to move it. But Moth squeezed herself tight and made her mind into a needle-sharp point of power.

She nodded, and the light fairies jumped up and down in place, varying the height of their jumps. Mother Dove seemed to be aflame. The wind added to the realism, blowing the fire this way and that.

The flame symbolised Mother Dove's origin as a magic bird.

She'd begun as an ordinary dove back when Neverland was an ordinary island. Then the volcano on Torth Mountain had erupted.

Grasslands burned. Forests burned. Animals died.

And Neverland woke up.

The dove's tree was the last to catch fire. Neverland noticed the tree and the dove, and decided that the dove could help the island.

The bird burned along with her tree. She burned, but she wasn't hurt. Her feathers weren't even singed.

She was changed, nonetheless. She became Mother Dove, and gained wisdom she'd had no inkling of before. A day later she laid her egg. A week later she molted, and the next day the fairies came, flying in short hops and glowing no brighter than a stone in sunlight.

Mother Dove loved them straight off, and she told them how to use the Molt. That had been the beginning, too many years ago to count.

Moth relaxed. The light fairies stopped jumping and lowered their glow. Fairies crowded around, congratulating them.

Mother Dove saw Tink and cooed to her. The coo was carried away by the wind, but Tink noticed Mother Dove's eye on her and came over.

When Tink said she didn't know where Prilla was, Mother Dove asked her to look for the child. "And if she isn't here, try the Home Tree. I'd hate for her to miss everything."

Tink was furious. Prilla could be anywhere, and Tink wanted to monitor how the repaired ladle was performing. She pushed through the revellers, wondering how she'd gotten saddled with Prilla.

The next event was Queen Ree's speech. Mother Dove sat up her tallest, and Ree perched on her head, just as she always did.

"Fairies," she began, shouting over the wind. "Sparrow men!"

"Louder!" several fairies yelled.

"Fairies, sparrow men, it has been ..." She hesitated. She wanted to say, as usual, that it had been a spectacular year. But it hadn't been. Too many fairies had died of disbelief. "It has been a good year."

"Louder!"

A raindrop fell on Ree's head, pushing her tiara down on her forehead and soaking her hair. A drop fell into Tink's ladle and sloshed purple punch on a fairy's chartreuse sleeve. Seven raindrops landed on Rani, drenching her completely. She laughed, loving it.

Thunder rumbled.

Everyone heard it. Rani stopped laughing. Mother Dove's pre-Molt tingle faded away.

There hadn't been a thunderstorm since before Mother Dove laid her egg.

There had never been a hurricane.

TWELVE

Queen Ree flew to face Mother Dove, who said, "Send everyone home while they can still fly."

Ree had no intention of obeying. Mother Dove was in danger, and her fairies wouldn't desert her. Ree turned and found Tink at her side. The queen issued instructions.

Tink picked a dozen of the fairies who were pressing in toward Mother Dove. They stationed themselves at intervals around the nest. After shaking a little fairy dust onto the nest, they began to lift it off its branch. The plan was to lower the nest and place it under a log, out of the wind.

But before they had raised it an inch, a gust rolled through and blew away Tink, her helpers, and the nest's outermost twigs. Beck saved herself by hugging Mother Dove's neck. Ree was above the wind, but her shoes were blown off.

A second squad of fairies surrounded the nest. But a bigger gust got them, and Ree and Beck as well. Only Mother Dove herself, who was twenty times the weight of a fairy, kept her place.

In the fairy circle, a lantern went over and set off a small blaze. Two fairies doused it with pitcher after pitcher of punch. Meanwhile, the cooking-talent fairies began wrapping up their things as fast as they could. Bess hugged her painting close and tried to battle the wind. A nursing-talent sparrow man tended a fairy who'd been slammed into a tree.

More fairies surged toward Mother Dove, but before they reached her, a fresh wind barrelled through, a wind that made the others seem gentle. In a wink it swept away every last fairy.

The hurricane had arrived.

Mother Dove cried for the fairies and begged for mercy for her egg.

The hurricane tossed giant boulders about as though they were ping-pong balls. It slammed Tink into a birch tree at the edge of the fairy circle. She slid down the trunk, the breath knocked out of her.

Not far from the fairy circle, Rani was caught by an updraft and borne above the canopy of trees. Then the wind veered, and she fell.

It would have been the end of her if a branch hadn't caught one of the wing slits of her dress. She was saved, but she couldn't free herself. She dangled, lurching this way and that in the wind, praying that her branch would hold.

The wind carried Queen Ree a mile beyond Fairy Haven.

It blew her into a tree hole and stopped up the opening with a lost boy's leather shoe. Ree squirmed into the shoe and pushed against the sole. It didn't budge. She rammed it with her shoulder. It still didn't budge.

She pushed aside the laces. Then she sat on the edge of the shoe and tried to ignore the smell. She wondered if the shoe was being held in place by the wind, or if it was wedged in so tight she'd never get out.

The hurricane tore a mast off the pirate ship and blew the ship out to sea. A mermaid was catapulted fifty feet up the beach, and her friends had to dive to the ocean floor for safety. Inland, even the dragon Kyto cowered in his prison cave.

Beck skimmed along the ground. She tried to stop, but she was less than an eyelash in the storm. She could feel Mother Dove's distress and was desperate to help her.

The wind blew Beck into a burrow. She sat up, bruised and scraped, and faced a clutch of terrified baby moles. Her mind reached out to them. There, there, she thought. It's all right.

She couldn't leave them.

There, there. You'll be fine. We'll be fine.

She wondered, But will we?

Terence found himself rolling down a slope, along with

grass and stones. Below surged a river of mud. If he kept going he'd be swallowed up. He thrust himself toward a tree root and was able to grab it with one arm. He got the other arm around it and hung on, trying to keep his head up, trying to breathe in air and not mud.

And all the while he worried about Tink.

At the birch tree, Tink got her breath back. She was too wet to fly, so she ran, hunched over, trying to get below the wind. She couldn't see Mother Dove's hawthorn, but she knew where it was.

She was halfway across the fairy circle when the hurricane sent another wind. This wind picked up a copper saucepan and thwacked her on the head with it. She passed out and was whisked out of the circle along with the fairy-dust sacks, the tablecloths, and Bess's portrait of Mother Dove.

THIRTEEN

*P*RILLA WAS AWAKENED by a deep groan. The Home Tree was swaying like an upside-down pendulum and groaning while it swayed. She flew to her window, but the wind had plastered a wet leaf across it.

The celebration!

She hurried down to the Home Tree's lobby and pulled open the door.

Her glow illuminated just a few inches, and she saw only rain, sheets of rain, almost no space between the drops. Lightning flashed. She gasped. The oak tree was gone! Gone! A hole where the roots had been.

She thought, Mother Dove! Tink! Rani! Terence! How could they be safe when the oak had been uprooted?

The world went dark again. Prilla knew she couldn't fly in this weather, and she knew she was probably safest where she was. She waited for another lightning flash.

It came, with a crack that nearly deafened her. She saw, off to her right, a path toward Mother Dove, a long distance on foot. She started out, and the wind shoved her back in.

She waited, then put her hand out. The wind had lessened, but as soon as it rose again she'd be blown away. She waited for more lightning.

It came, and she saw, not far off, a rock to shelter under. She left the lobby and was drenched instantly. She almost slipped and kicked off her roll-back shoes as she raced for the rock.

She made it, just ahead of the wind. She crouched and waited for light and less wind. The lightning flashed. She saw raised tree roots that she might reach on her next sprint. The wind weakened, and she ran.

Mother Dove's hawthorn had been stripped of its leaves, but Mother Dove remained untouched. At first she'd been terrified. If she died, her beloved fairies would lose their fairy dust. If her beloved egg cracked, the animals and people would age and die, and she would, too.

But as the hours passed, and the wind whipped above and below her, she relaxed, believing that Neverland was protecting her.

She was right. The island was protecting her, but it was a struggle. The hurricane was determined to do its worst, and the worst would be wiping out Mother Dove and her egg.

The hurricane sent its fiercest winds and its heaviest rain

at the nest, without a moment for rest. The island held out bravely, pressing back the storm, determined not to give way.

But when the frontal assault failed, the hurricane changed its strategy. It moved its strongest winds out to sea and stirred up a wave big enough to drown the entire island.

Of course, Neverland had to dodge the wave. It marshalled its forces.

The moment Neverland's attention was diverted, the hurricane dispatched a vicious gale that scooped Mother Dove off her nest.

She battled the wind to get back to her egg. She beat her wings against it, pecked it, butted it with her head. But she was only blown farther away. She exhausted herself and had no strength left when the storm lifted her high above the island and slammed her down on the shore.

She lay on the beach, her chest caved in, both wings broken.

At least her egg was still unharmed. She was sure she'd know if anything happened to it, no matter how far away she was.

In fact, the wind that had taken her had whistled by the egg without cracking it. It still rested serenely in the nest, as smooth as ever, as peacefully blue as ever. A full minute passed. Then lightning snaked down, splitting the shell, and incinerating the egg.

A shudder ran through the island. Mother Dove felt it and knew what it meant.

My egg! she thought. Oh, my egg! The magic she'd been given – the best of her, her gift to the island – was destroyed. She wailed into the wind.

FOURTEEN

*A*FTER SHATTERING THE EGG, the storm weakened. The rain diminished. The wind slackened. The sky brightened toward dawn.

Tink woke up. She was facedown on a broken porcelain plate, and it was a wonder she had no cuts. Her head throbbed. She put her hand to her forehead and felt a bump the size of a peppercorn. She probed it and bit her lip to keep from crying out. *What happened?* she thought.

She sat up. Her memory came back. She jumped up, and fell over, her head spinning. She had to find Mother Dove. Tink stood up more carefully and began to walk, scanning the sky for hawks. She was out of fairy dust, so she couldn't really fly. But she fluttered her wings, flew short hops, and ran in between.

She hurried through a field of flattened bamboo littered with branches, rocks, and the pirate ship's mast. She passed a bewildered squirrel and a lark with bloody tail feathers. She called out to the lark that she'd try to find an animal-talent fairy.

Everywhere fairies were putting themselves and one another to rights. Queen Ree managed to push the shoe out of the tree hole she was stuck in. A scout heard Rani's cries and freed her from the branch. The baby moles' mother returned to her burrow, and Beck was able to leave. Terence finally let go of the root. He was covered in mud, but he was alive.

The first to find Mother Dove was Prilla. Halfway to the fairy circle, Prilla had fallen into Havendish Stream. She'd have drowned if the current hadn't been so strong. It had carried her to the beach, where she'd climbed up onto a sand dune. When the sky had lightened, she'd seen Mother Dove.

She rushed across the sand. Mother Dove's wings rested at odd angles, and her feathers were caked with sand. But Prilla thought her eyes were the worst, sunken and defeated.

Mother Dove cooed, "Prilla..."

Prilla was crying, tears streaming down her cheeks.

Mother Dove's voice was almost too soft to hear. "Prilla... I thought you might come."

"Oh, Mother Dove... Oh..."

Perhaps it was Prilla's youth, or perhaps it was Prilla's shoulders, which refused to slump even while she wept – but Mother Dove began to believe that something might yet be done for her poor egg. And if her egg were whole again and she were reunited with it, she thought she might be healed as well.

She delved into her store of wisdom and island lore. She concluded that there really was a chance.

Since the egg had begun by fire and had been undone by fire, it might be restored by fire. But the fire would have to be very hot – an inferno. Where would such a fire be found? Torth Mountain hadn't erupted in centuries.

There was the dragon Kyto.

But why would he help?

Mother Dove's chest heaved. "Find Queen Ree and Beck and bring them to me."

Prilla nodded and ran, speeding herself up by quick bursts of flight. Mother Dove closed her eyes and thought.

Prilla was halfway to Fairy Haven when she met Beck, limping toward the beach. Prilla pointed the way to Mother Dove and ran on.

She found Ree with Tink, who was holding a chunk of ice to her forehead. The queen's tiara had been blown off, but Prilla knew her by her erect posture, the set of her head, and her penetrating gaze.

She and Tink were perched on a branch above the ruined egg. The blackened shell had broken into three pieces. Cradled in the largest piece was a thimbleful of ashes, the remains of the egg.

"Mother Dove wouldn't have left her egg," Tink said.

Ree nodded. "The scouts are searching. But…"

The two of them imagined all the disasters that could have overcome Mother Dove.

Prilla started climbing the hawthorn.

"Even if Mother Dove's all right now," Tink said, "she won't be when she sees the egg."

Prilla reached them. She curtsied to Ree – although Never fairies never curtsied – and told them about Mother Dove.

The three of them hurried to the beach, where Beck was weeping and stroking Mother Dove's wing feathers. Ree wept, too, and even Tink broke down.

Prilla, who had cried herself out, hoped she had a talent for helping after a hurricane.

Ree said, "Are you in pain?"

Mother Dove whispered, "Not much."

But Beck knew that Mother Dove's pain was terrible.

"There will be no Molt," Mother Dove whispered. "I'm too weak."

Ree's mind reeled. No Molt! No Molt meant no fairy dust – no magic, no safety from hawks, no safety at all.

Mother Dove said, "I might get well if the egg..." Her voice wavered. "...were restored and it was with me again."

But it's cracked and burned, Prilla thought.

Tink thought, I've fixed pots almost as bad as the egg.

"How?" Beck asked.

"It will be difficult." Mother Dove explained, using as few words as possible.

When Mother Dove was finished, Ree told Beck and Prilla

and Tink to send all the fairies to her, here on the beach.

Mother Dove whispered, "Don't go, Tink. I want you to stay with me. Ree, I'm sure there are other injured animals besides me. Have Beck help some of them."

Beck staggered back.

"Beck..." Mother Dove cooed a long string of coos.

Beck felt Mother Dove's love, but she didn't understand why Mother Dove didn't want her.

"We're too weepy, Beck," Mother Dove said. "Both of us. We'll make each other sadder and sadder." She knew Beck's heart would break if she stayed.

Beck nodded. But she still wished she could stay.

Tink pulled her bangs. She had no idea how to care for Mother Dove. "I'll do my best."

Beck and Prilla left the beach to round up the other fairies.

While they were busy, the sky cleared, and the sun rose. The pirate ship sailed back into Pirate Cove. The beached mermaid made her slow way back to the sea.

The animals and Clumsies of the island began to feel the loss of the egg. A Never bear, who'd slept through the storm, woke to find his left knee feeling stiff. Captain Hook looked in his mirror to shave and found a grey hair among his black locks.

Peter Pan woke up in a meadow where the storm had dropped him. He was horrified to see a baby tooth on the grass next to his head. It was his first tooth to fall out, and it hadn't even been loose yesterday.

The fairies were slow to assemble since they couldn't fly. Some were bandaged, some were limping. A sparrow man had been blinded. Two fairies were missing. One had been blown out to sea, and one had died of disbelief during the night.

Terence stood at the edge of the crowd of fairies. He was still muddy. Even his teeth were brownish when he showed them in a big smile. Although he felt sad about Mother Dove, he couldn't help showing his relief that Tink was safe.

She didn't see the smile.

Ree began her speech with the news that Mother Dove was too injured to molt. "But all may be well if her egg is restored and brought to her. I will send a fairy on a quest to restore the egg and bring it here."

Prilla imagined being selected and turning out to have an egg-saving talent.

Ree went on. "The fairy will take much of the remaining fairy dust. I'll keep only enough for our scouts."

Everyone but the scouts grumbled.

Ree held up her hand. "Even so, we have only a few days' supply left."

Each fairy imagined life without flying or magic. Would they still be fairies or just a kind of pale glowworm?

FIFTEEN

*V*IDIA WISHED she'd had time to pluck more feathers. She had only a few handfuls left of fresh dust. "Dear hearts, we should pluck Mother Dove now. If we wait until she dies, her feathers will probably have no power at all."

Prilla was horrified, along with almost everybody else. But several fairies thought the suggestion worth considering. If they plucked Mother Dove, they'd have enough dust for a year.

Mother Dove knew Vidia was right. Her feathers would lose their power if she died. But if it comes to that, she thought, when I'm dying, I'll tell them to pluck me.

Tink said, "Anyone who comes plucking will have to get by me first."

"Me, too," Terence said.

Me, too! Prilla thought.

Ree said, "Shame on you, Vidia. No one will pluck Mother Dove. We will put our trust in the quest."

Prilla wondered if she could follow the quester secretly, in case someone was needed in an emergency.

"Now," Ree said, "I want everyone to look over the damage to your talent places and report to me at the Home

Tree." She dismissed everyone except Rani.

"Me?" Rani felt honoured. She blew her nose on a leafkerchief.

Mother Dove whispered, "Prilla, too."

"Prilla?" Ree said. "She's so young."

"Prilla. And Vidia."

"Vidia!"

Mother Dove nodded. "For her speed."

Ree called to them, and they returned. Prilla was astonished to be chosen. She wondered if it meant the queen saw a talent in her. The quest would be such an adventure, and she'd be having the adventure with Rani, her favourite fairy.

Ree seated herself on a driftwood branch, and Rani joined her. Prilla sat on the sand nearby, a few feet from Tink, who was kneeling and brushing sand out of Mother Dove's feathers.

Mother Dove wished Tink would stop. Tink kept jostling Mother Dove's wings, which made the pain worse.

Vidia stood apart. "I'm not so dreadful when you need me, am I, dar – "

Rani finished the word. " – lings. There's good in everyone, I think."

Ree said, "You've all heard of Kyto, haven't you?"

Prilla shook her head.

"Kyto is a dragon," Rani explained. "A fiery dragon." She wiped sweat off her forehead.

He was imprisoned in a cave high in Torth Mountain, which rises from the center of the island. He'd been caught when he was still young by the lost boys and the fairy queen before Ree.

Ree said, "Mother Dove believes that the egg can be healed by fire, if the fire is hot enough. Kyto's fire – "

Rani finished the sentence. " – is hot enough."

"Won't the fire cook the egg?" Prilla asked.

"Not my egg," Mother Dove whispered proudly. "It would cook an ordinary egg."

Vidia said, "Sweeties, do you think Kyto will heal the egg out of kindness?"

"He's not kind!" Rani said.

Vidia smiled her most irritating smile. "I know, dear."

"He's wicked," Mother Dove whispered. "Don't trust him."

Kyto was utterly wicked. Even Captian Hook's villainy paled in comparison. Kyto's capacity for mischief was unbounded, and there wasn't a shred of kindness in him.

"Won't Kyto want to save the egg?" Prilla asked. "Didn't it keep him young, too?"

"No," Ree said. "Mother Dove says the egg had no effect on him."

"Darlings, freedom is the only thing that will interest – "

Rani jumped in. " – him. But we shouldn't free him, should we?"

"No!" Ree said. "It would be too dangerous. Besides, fairies aren't strong enough to do it. Mother Dove says he may restore the egg, even without a promise of freedom, if we give him some things for his hoard."

"What's a hoard?" Prilla asked.

"Dragons are collectors," Ree said. "A hoard is a dragon's collection of beautiful and unusual objects. It's as dear to him as his – "

" – flame." Rani frowned. "What do we have that Kyto would want?"

"Nothing," Ree said. "You have to get the items first."

"Naturally," Vidia said.

"What items?" Rani asked.

Mother Dove had thought hard about this. Dragons prize gold and jewels, but they prize rarities even more. The more difficult a thing is to come by, the more they want it. Mother Dove had decided on three items that were likely to tempt Kyto.

Ree said, "A feather from the golden hawk – "

Vidia laughed bitterly. "It's fine to pluck the golden hawk, who'll kill us – but not Mother Dove."

Mother Dove whispered, "It's not fine to pluck anyone. But it must be done."

Ree continued. "Captain Hook's silver double cigar holder, and a mermaid's comb. Those are the things."

Silence fell. It would take a miracle to get even one of them.

SIXTEEN

R EE WOULDN'T let the questers start out until they'd slept a few hours and eaten a decent meal.

Rani dreamed her usual dream, of swimming. Her wings became flippers, and her lungs became gills. Fish circled around her. Mermaids let her join their festivities. After hours of revelry, she rose, up, up, up, and out of the water. Her flippers became wings again. She flew over the lagoon, her flight as exhilarating as her swim.

She woke up crying. She'd never swim, never enter the ocean's realm. After she dried her eyes, she changed into her dress with six pockets and tucked a leafkerchief into each one.

In her sour-plum-tree home, Vidia dreamed of flying through a cloud of fairy dust. When she woke up, she opened the seven locks to the strongbox under her bed and took out the pouch that held her remaining fresh dust. She hung the pouch on her belt and tucked it into her skirt so that the bulge didn't show.

Prilla's dreams again took her through the dreams of Clumsy children. The last dream – a sweet one that took place in a sweet shop – clung to her when she awoke, and it took her a few seconds to remember where she was.

The quest! The quest to restore the egg, and her own quest to discover her talent. She leaped out of bed and dressed quickly. She hoped the spaghetti laces on her boots weren't too flimsy to last.

She pinned a swatch of her Arrival Garment inside her collar, just to have something familiar. She wished she had a stuffed animal or a doll to take. But there were no such things in Neverland.

The questers dined in the tearoom with Ree. They were served dwarf mushroom caps filled with sesame-seed puree, the first food the kitchen had ever cooked without fairy dust. The mushrooms were half raw, and the puree was too salty, but only Vidia noticed.

Night had fallen. Prilla saw a full moon through the tearoom window.

Vidia said, "Ree, my love, how are we going to carry the broken egg from place to – "

" – place?" Rani wished she'd thought of this. "And what about the quest items?" The cigar holder and the comb would be heavy.

Ree said she would leave the egg for them at the fairy circle. "The carpenter-talent fairies are building a shed. The egg will be in there. You can store each quest item as you get it, and collect everything at the end."

"*If* we get everything," Vidia said. "If we get *anything*. Sweeties, we should pluck Mother Dove now, before she croaks." She enjoyed the shock on the others' faces.

Ree didn't bother to scold her. She just added, "I'll give you a balloon carrier to use when you go to Kyto."

Prilla wondered why Vidia was going on the quest if she was sure it would fail.

But Vidia wasn't sure it would fail, and she wanted it to succeed as much as the others did. Besides, she wanted to fly when other fairies couldn't, and she wanted to keep her supply of fresh dust in reserve.

Rani suggested they go after Captain Hook's double cigar holder first.

"Love, how do you plan to take it away from him?"

"Won't he be sleeping?" Prilla asked.

"Dear child, he never takes the cigar holder out of his – "

" – mouth. That's only a rumour."

Ree said, "Perhaps you can pull it out without waking him."

Prilla hoped she could do it and show a talent for pulling out cigar holders. Or a general talent for pirates.

After the meal, Ree escorted them to the lobby, where a throng waited to see them off. Terence stood at the entrance with a satchel slung over his shoulder.

Ree said, "Terence has four days of dust for each of you, and I'm keeping four days for the scouts. In five days, our dust will be gone." Her voice caught. "And I fear Mother Dove will be gone by then, too."

Tears began to pour down Rani's cheeks.

Prilla was sad, too, but she was also excited. Her life was beginning. She was on her way to save Mother Dove and find her talent.

Ree had the nagging feeling she needed to do something.

Terence dipped into the satchel. He ceremoniously sprinkled a cup – not a particle more nor a particle less – of fairy dust on each quester. "Three days remain," he said.

He tightened the satchel's drawstring and held the satchel out. Vidia reached for it. He drew back.

Ree realised what she had to do. She had to name Rani leader, or Vidia would take over. Rani wasn't ideal. She was too gushy and eager to please. But Prilla was a complete unknown, really just a newborn.

Ree had considered going herself, but Mother Dove hadn't chosen her. "Rani, I want you to lead the – "

" – quest? Me?" Rani wondered if she was up to the job. "Thank you for your faith in me."

Prilla thought, Rani's awfully nice, but is she a leader?

"Vidia..." the queen said. "Vidia, look at me."

"Yes, dearest." Vidia looked up.

"The quest won't succeed if you make trouble."

"Make trouble, dearest?"

"I want you to accept Rani as your leader."

"Yes, dearest."

"And help her."

"Yes, dearest."

"And be good to Prilla."

"Yes, dearest."

"Mmm…" Ree knew Vidia's promises were worth little, but she didn't know what more to do. She told Terence to give the dust satchel to Rani.

He lifted it over Rani's head and adjusted the strap across her shoulder.

They were ready to go.

"Wait!" Tink pushed through the crowd. "Here." She gave Rani her favourite dagger (once a pirate's toothpick). "I have another one." She touched her second-best dagger in its sheath at her waist.

Ree intoned, "Questers, be careful, be kind, be a Never fairy at her best."

They were off.

SEVENTEEN

*T*HE QUESTERS started for Pirate Cove.

Prilla said, "We're sort of a talent, aren't we? We're quest-talent – "

" – fairies." Rani felt sorry for Prilla. "A talent is a little different."

"Entirely different," Vidia said. "For example, dear child, you always like and care about the others in your talent."

That's mean! Prilla thought.

"Vidia!" Rani said. "We care about each other."

"I care about Rani," Prilla said pointedly.

Rani blew her nose, touched.

"Dear child, I don't mind if you hate me. But let's see if I care about you. Let's see if your talent is fast-flying." Vidia sped up and called over her shoulder, "Catch me."

Prilla fluttered her wings as hard as she could. She kicked her feet and flapped her arms. She didn't want to be in anything with Vidia, but she wanted to outdo her. And, of course, she wanted a talent.

She wished a wind would come along and push her, only her.

But no wind came, and no matter what she did, she could fly just slightly faster than Rani. She had no chance of reaching Vidia, who was a dot in the distance.

Vidia waited for them at the shore. When they arrived, she said, "Dear child, your talent is for being untalented."

"Don't listen, Prilla," Rani said. "Vidia, we have no time for insults."

"Precious, we have no time for slowpokes." Vidia started out over the water.

They flew the three-quarters of a mile to the ship. The night was so quiet you could almost hear Neverland thinking. On the *Jolly Roger*, the helmsman nodded at his wheel.

The fairies flew from porthole to porthole, wondering which belonged to Captain Hook. They mistakenly flew through the crew's porthole window and were blown right back out by the snores.

Three portholes farther on, they entered Hook's cabin. Hook snored too, but his snores were refined. He snored in iambic pentameter, with an occasional spondee thrown in.

Prilla hovered above Hook's bureau, where a dozen roses had been placed exactly as he liked them – stems in water, with the decapitated blooms arranged around the vase.

Vidia touched down on his desk in the midst of his

collection of nose lengtheners.

Rani flew to the bed.

There, clenched in Hook's teeth, was the cigar holder, bearing two enormous unlit cigars.

Hook lay on his back. He'd thrown off his blanket, and his pillow was bunched beneath his large head. His hand rested on the sword strapped around his nightshirt. As Rani watched, he shifted a little and scratched his belly with his hook.

He stopped snoring and began to speak. Prilla froze in fright and almost fell out of the air.

"Captain Joshua Abreu, March sixth, 'twenty-two: planked."

His eyes didn't open, and the fairies realised he was talking in his sleep. The cigar holder moved as he spoke, but it didn't fall out.

"Captain John Amberding, July seventh, 'twenty-four: poisoned. Captain Harvey Ardill, October eighteenth, 'twenty: planked. Captain William Bault, January fifth, 'eighteen: planked."

Hook was listing the captains he'd killed, alphabetically!

How gruesome! Rani thought. Cold with fear, she flew to Hook's lips and pulled gently on the cigar holder.

It didn't budge.

"Captain Alistair Bested, February twenty-seventh,

GAIL CARSON LEVINE

'twenty-one: hooked and dangled."

Rani wondered if he'd start on the first mates when he finished the captains.

"What do we do now, sweet – "

" – heart?" Rani wished Ree had sent someone else to be leader. "Er... Er..."

"Captain Simon Bontarre, August..."

"Maybe if we wait awhile," Prilla said, "something will happen."

No one could think of anything better, so they settled themselves amid the roses on the bureau. Prilla felt proud of having made a suggestion that the others had followed. Rani tried to think of a way to get the cigar holder, but no ideas came.

And if they did get it, Rani wasn't sure they'd be able to carry it. The holder was five and a half inches long, studded with emeralds. Even without the two gigantic cigars it would be heavy. They'd use fairy dust to lighten both the cigars and the holder, but still, they'd have a job bringing it all to shore.

An hour passed while Hook recited dead captains up to the letter *H*.

Rani tried to drown him out by whistling mermaid songs. While she whistled she worried. They weren't going to save Mother Dove if they spent the next three days on Hook.

Vidia cracked her knuckles.

Prilla arrived in the bedroom of a Clumsy boy who was sitting up in bed, looking frightened.

"What's wrong?"

He whispered, "Something's breathing under the bed."

Prilla flew down to see. No monster, just a few dust bunnies.

"All clear." She did a handspring in the air –

And landed on the pillow of a girl who was reading under the covers with a flashlight. Prilla somersaulted onto the girl's ear. The girl didn't notice. Giggling, Prilla sang, "There's a fairy in your ear." The girl reached up, but –

Prilla was back on the ship. Hook was still clenching the cigar holder. She said, "Don't you love being silly with Clumsy children?"

"Dear child, why would I do that?" Vidia said.

"I've never tried it," Rani said.

Prilla wondered if she was doing something wrong by going to the mainland. She didn't go on purpose, but she'd be miserable if she stopped.

A second hour passed. Prilla visited the mainland again (a zoo and an ice-skating rink), but this time she didn't mention it.

Hook reached the letter *N*.

Vidia said, "Rani, darling, if you don't stop whistling, I'll rip your lips – "

" – off. I guess I'll stop."

Prilla had liked the whistling. And she thought a leader should stand up for herself.

A third hour passed. Dawn wasn't far off, and Hook would wake soon.

Once he woke up, they'd never get the holder.

EIGHTEEN

*T*INKER BELL spent the night at Mother Dove's side. Sometimes Mother Dove woke up, weeping for her egg. Each time, Tink patted her neck feathers awkwardly and said, "Don't cry. Try to sleep."

But Mother Dove couldn't not cry, although eventually she did go back to sleep. Only to wake up again. And again.

Another half hour passed on the pirate ship. Hook reached the letter *R*.

"Darlings, can't someone think of something?"

Vidia hasn't made any brilliant suggestions, Prilla thought. She said, "What if I tickle his feet? Maybe he'll let – "

" – go." Rani wiped her sweaty forehead. If Hook did let go, she wasn't sure she and Vidia could carry the cigar holder by themselves.

But what else was there to do? "Good idea," she said. "But wait until Vidia and I are ready."

Prilla flew to Hook's feet and saw the birthmark on his left instep – a cutlass dripping blood. Her wings stiffened with fear.

Rani and Vidia positioned themselves under the cigar holder. Prilla steeled herself and tickled.

But Hook wasn't ticklish.

Prilla flew to Rani, and the fairies hovered above Hook's face. Ooh, he's ugly! Prilla thought. His skin looked like candle wax.

"I want to try something," Rani said. "Go to the holder."

Prilla and Vidia went.

Rani flew to Hook's ear and shouted, "Open your mouth!" She knew he couldn't hear her, but sometimes a concept got through.

Nothing happened.

She shouted louder, every syllable slow and distinct. "OPEN YOUR MOUTH!" Please open, she thought, for Mother Dove and the fairies.

Nothing happened.

Rani found herself weeping. "Open your mouth, you bad pirate."

Nothing happened.

"Open your mouth, you murderer!" She kicked his cheek as hard as she could with her pointy-toed wasp-skin boots.

Ouch! Hook's mouth opened in surprise.

Vidia and Prilla pulled the cigar holder out.

Hook woke up. In a flash, his sword was out and he was on his feet, slicing the air. "Have at you, villain!" He smiled in the darkness. A new foe to kill.

The cigar holder was too heavy for Prilla and Vidia, although they tried to slow its fall. Rani wanted to fly over and help, but she was afraid of being sliced.

The cigar holder landed on the floor.

Hook felt no resistance to his sword. "Where are you, knave?" He lowered the weapon and peered into the darkness.

Rani flew down to the holder. She and Prilla shook fairy dust on it. Vidia might have added some of her fresh dust and made it even lighter. But she wanted to save her dust for herself.

Hook wondered if the jab at his cheek had been a dream. He sheathed his sword and noticed the cigar holder wasn't in his mouth.

Vidia and Rani tilted the holder while Prilla pulled on a cigar.

Hook saw the holder and reached down for it. It jerked as Prilla got the cigar out. When he saw the cigar and the holder move, Hook stumbled back. A ghost! He felt a cold draft waft through the open cabin door.

But he feared no man, living or dead. "Spirit, back to Davy Jones's locker!" He drew his sword again, stabbing here and stabbing there. He raked the air with his hook.

The fairies were afraid to move. The open porthole looked miles away.

In a downward sweep of his sword, Hook accidentally lopped off one of Rani's pockets.

Someone has to distract him, Prilla thought. Even though she was terrified, she ran around him. Staying close to his nightshirt, she flew up to his head where she pulled on one of his corkscrew curls, as hard as she could.

He whirled around. "Coward, face me!"

Rani and Vidia shook the cigar holder, and the second cigar fell out. Even without the cigars, the holder was heavy, but they began to fly it upward, toward the porthole. Prilla kept pulling Hook's hair.

He stabbed and still felt nothing against his sword. He whirled again and saw the holder, on its way to the porthole. Two ghosts! he thought. One pulling my hair and one stealing my cigar holder.

He dropped his sword and reached for the ghost pulling his hair. With his hook he attacked the air where the other ghost should have been.

Rani and Vidia flew through the porthole.

Hook's hand closed around Prilla.

NINETEEN

*H*OOK WATCHED his cigar holder vanish over the waves. When it was gone he looked down at his fist. Prilla's head was free, but he couldn't see it. Nonetheless, he knew he'd caught something, and he didn't think it was a ghost.

His grip was too firm for Prilla to wriggle out. Her wings were crumpled. She'd have been in agony if wings felt pain.

Hook wanted light to see what he was holding. He headed for his lantern. As he walked, he tightened his grip on Prilla. The pressure on her lungs was so great she couldn't even scream.

Not that screaming would do any good.

Out over the ocean, Rani felt awful about leaving Prilla behind. Naturally, they'd come back for her; but she could be dead by then.

The cigar holder grew heavier with every inch. Despite their frantic efforts, she and Vidia were descending.

The holder would have been much lighter if Vidia had used her fresh dust before. She wasn't thinking about that, however, because she never blamed herself for anything. Instead, she was mad at Rani for not flying faster.

The shore was a half mile off, and at this rate they'd never get there with the holder.

Prilla wished she had Rani's dagger. She wished she were covered with butter. She wished she could vanish and reappear wherever Rani and Vidia were.

Hook started lighting the lantern with his teeth and his hook. He'd done it many times. It took only a few minutes.

Prilla began to hope. He'd open his hand to look at her, and when he did, she'd fly away – if her wings still worked.

Rani and Vidia were eighteen inches above the waves. They'd been graced with a strong wind at their backs, and they hadn't lost any height for a few minutes.

But Rani was tiring rapidly.

Hook got the lantern lit. He went to the porthole and shut the window. Then he started for the door.

Prilla was going to be trapped.

Rani and Vidia were fighting a downdraft that had forced them within nine inches of the water. Vidia had already felt ocean spray on her ankles.

❋

Hook was three steps from his door. Prilla bit into his index finger as hard as she could. She spat out the blood, which was viscous and purple and tasted like spoiled cheese. She bit again. And again.

Veteran of many battles, Hook was accustomed to pain. He took two more dogged steps before he looked down at his hand –

And saw his own blood. A ticking crocodile and the sight of his purple blood were all Hook feared. He shrieked and let go of Prilla.

Before she hit the floor, her wings righted themselves, and she began to fly. She flew out of the cabin, up a short flight of stairs to the deck, and over the ocean, hurrying after Rani and Vidia.

The sea was vast. Prilla looked for Rani's and Vidia's glows, but the sky was brightening, and fairy glow no longer stood out.

Still, Prilla thought she saw a sparkle. She flew toward it, hoping it wasn't Rani and Vidia. If it was, they were very close to the water. Prilla flew faster, although she was exhausted by her struggle with Hook.

She shouted, "I'm coming! Don't drown!" But her voice was lost in the roar of the waves.

The shore was a quarter mile off. Rani and Vidia

descended another inch.

Prilla was catching up, but not fast enough.

Rani wondered if it was time to tell Vidia to drop the holder and save herself.

They descended another inch.

Rani yelled, "Drop the holder!" although she didn't let go.

Vidia was as brave as Rani. She yelled, "No!"

Rani thought of drowning, of melting into the delicious sea.

Prilla yelled, "I'm coming!"

But it was hopeless. She couldn't possibly reach them in time.

TWENTY

*T*HE QUEST would have ended right then. Rani and Vidia and possibly Prilla would have drowned.

But Neverland interceded.

The island had been observing the fairies and rooting for them. It didn't want them to fail.

So it slid the beach toward them.

When Rani and Vidia fell into the sea, expecting to die, the water came up only to their knees.

A wave was coming. They dragged themselves and the holder onto dry sand. But they couldn't remain there either. It would be absurd to escape drowning only to be killed by a hawk. They pulled the holder toward an outcropping of rock a few yards up the beach. Prilla arrived and helped.

Then they collapsed.

A cool autumn breeze swept across the island, although autumn had never before come to Neverland, only spring and summer.

Peter Pan woke to find a dozen baby teeth next to him on his sleeping mat.

Hook's bosun, Smee, couldn't remember where he'd left his spectacles.

The Never bear's knee was stiffer today. And when he sniffed the air, he smelled a beehive but couldn't tell if it was to his north or to his south.

In the courtyard outside the Home Tree, Queen Ree shivered in her open-weave fern mantle. A sparrow man ran to her. All over Fairy Haven, nuts had ripened overnight and had fallen to the ground.

At first Ree thought that was good, but then she realised that the mill wouldn't grind without dust. They were likely to starve.

Still half asleep, Mother Dove wondered why she didn't feel the egg under her. Then she remembered, and her heart broke all over again.

Her eyes had filmed over during the night. Everything looked blurry. She swung her head, searching for Tink.

"I'm here." Tink made herself smile to keep from crying.

Mother Dove whispered, "Talk to me."

Tink had no idea what to say. Then she thought of the pots and pans on her worktable. "Dulcie brought in a cookie cutter last week. Won't cut any shape but clover. She tried ..."

If she'd been well, Mother Dove would have been glad to

listen to whatever Tink wanted to say about a cookie cutter. But now she couldn't keep her mind on the words. "Not about cookie cutters, Tink. Or pots."

Not about pots? But Tink didn't have anything else to talk about. She thought for a full five minutes. She took out her dagger and turned it over and over in her hands.

Then she began, "The first time I met Peter Pan I saved him from a shark." She'd never told this to anyone. She'd never talked about Peter before.

Better, Mother Dove thought. She settled herself as comfortably as she could and willed herself to listen.

In the early afternoon, Prilla awoke from dreaming the dreams of Clumsy children. Rani and Vidia were still asleep, and she was afraid to wake them. Vidia would probably make a crack about a talent for waking fairies up when they wanted to sleep.

Prilla sighed. She decided to see if she could blink over to the mainland on purpose. She was probably misbehaving, but it was such fun to be there, and she didn't see what harm it did.

She closed her eyes and remembered the bedroom of the boy who'd heard noises under his bed. A bicycle had leaned against one wall. A window had been open. The curtains had been blue and white stripes. She tried to push herself there.

She tried to take a gigantic leap.

Her eyes opened. She hadn't budged an inch.

She closed her eyes again and pictured a tunnel. In her mind she flew through it. She imagined cold stone walls, a rounded ceiling, a muddy floor. She stayed a while in the tunnel, getting to know it. At the other end, she told herself, was the mainland.

She thought her strategy was succeeding. She thought she'd left Neverland.

She opened her eyes. Next to her, Rani rolled onto her side.

Prilla hadn't gone anywhere, but, although she didn't know it, she had made a beginning.

TWENTY-ONE

*T*INK FELL silent. She'd never felt so tired, and all she'd done was tell stories. She'd told Mother Dove about the adventures she'd had with Peter and about their friendship. She'd said how he used to tell her his jokes and ideas, and she'd admired every one. Extravagantly. She'd admired them extravagantly.

Of course, Peter hadn't reciprocated. He wasn't much of a listener, or much of an admirer of anything that didn't come from him.

Tink had even admitted to Mother Dove that she'd neglected her pots and pans for Peter. She hadn't said to Mother Dove, "I loved him," but her meaning had been tantamount to saying so.

"His hair was so silky," she'd said. "I used to perch on his head, just to feel it. And his nose! I could tell if he was smiling by looking at nothing but his nose. It would flatten when he smiled and wrinkle when he laughed. And when he wasn't smiling or laughing, it was as nice as a frying pan."

There was little left to tell, only the bit that made her feel the most betrayed. She didn't want to tell it. It was too embarrassing and too painful.

"Go on," Mother Dove said.

Tink tugged on her bangs. "But it's sad," she said, hoping she wouldn't have to continue.

"Go on," Mother Dove said. How sad could anything be, compared to the egg?

Tink nodded. "That first day, after I saved him from the shark, I showed him my workshop. I showed him everything. I fixed a pot while he watched." Tears streamed down Tink's cheeks. It could have happened yesterday, that's how much it hurt.

"When I was done ..." She had to stop and take a few deep breaths. "When I was finished fixing the pot, he said ..." She hiccupped. "He said, 'How clever I am to pick the very best fairy.'" Tink faced away from Mother Dove and sobbed.

"He couldn't have meant it," Tink continued while weeping. "If he really thought I was the best, why did he bring over the Wendy?" She collapsed on the sand, still sobbing. "Why did he spend all his time with her?"

Mother Dove was momentarily taken outside herself. Oh, my, she thought. Tink has carried that a long while. Poor Tink.

Rani and Vidia didn't wake up until the sun was setting.

"Dear child," Vidia said, "how could you let us sleep so

long? Do you think we have time to waste? Do you think?"

Even Rani said Prilla might have used better judgment.

Prilla thought sadly that judgment was another talent she didn't seem to have.

The three of them carried the cigar holder to the shed at the fairy circle. As Ree had promised, the egg was there, along with a balloon carrier, a low-sided wagon held aloft by dust-filled balloons. A cord was attached to the wagon, so a fairy could pull it along.

The queen had also left a surprise in the shed, a fig-chocolate cake that had been baked before the hurricane. It had been freshly iced, however. The icing was white with red letters that said, *Congratulations on your first success!*

Rani said they'd go to the hawk next. It was the obvious choice, because the lagoon is dangerous at night. The mermaids do their deepest singing then. Clumsies have been driven mad by the sound, and fairies have been turned into bats. Even fish avoid the lagoon at night.

On the other hand, night was the sensible time to go to the hawk, who'd be away hunting during the day. Rani lifted the dust satchel strap over her head. She opened the satchel and sprinkled dust on each of them.

Two days of dust remained.

The distance from the fairy circle to the river depended on

the size of Neverland. Tonight the island was large, so the questers faced a long flight.

They flew over a banana-tree forest, which the hurricane had savaged. They flew over a village of tiffens, the banana farmers. Tiffens, who have ears like an elephant's, are half the size of Clumsies. They don't come into this tale, but the fairies trade with them.

It was cold. Prilla and Vidia swung their arms and kicked to stay warm. Rani was hot as usual and wiped her neck with a leafkerchief.

Vidia flew backward for a while, watching the other two. "Darlings," she said, "you use your wings so ridiculously, it's a miracle you can fly at all."

Neither Prilla nor Rani bothered to answer. They were both worrying about Mother Dove. Prilla hoped Mother Dove wasn't too cold. Rani hoped she was drinking enough liquids. They both refused to think that Mother Dove might already have died. But the fear floated at the edge of their thoughts.

The golden hawk tired easily since the egg's destruction. When it grew dark, he was glad to return to his nest atop an upright stone in a line of stones on the other side of the wide Wough River.

Vidia remembered all the hawks she'd seen, diving out of the sky, hardly slowing before they pounced on their hapless prey. She wished she could dive like that.

The golden hawk had flown disgracefully low all day, because he was worried about diving. He feared he'd crash.

Rani had heard that the golden hawk had a magic eye. He fixed you with that eye and you lost the will to move. You were half dead by the time he sank his talons into you.

The golden hawk's vision was failing. Ordinarily he could fly as high as a cloud and still count the blades of grass below. But today all he saw was a green blur. Even worse, he had twice mistaken rocks for rabbits.

Prilla wondered how it would feel to be eaten and how long it would be before she died.

He'd finally pounced on a squirrel. But it had shaken him off by swishing its tail across his face. Then it had scampered away.

He'd never been so humiliated.

After three hours, the questers reached the river and began to follow it upstream. Vidia, who was flying ahead, saw the standing stones in a meadow surrounded by pine trees.

The questers descended into the treetops and approached cautiously.

And there was the hawk, a commanding silhouette against the starry sky.

There was the hawk, wide awake, chilled to the bone, terrified of falling off his stone.

TWENTY-TWO

SINCE SHE'D told Mother Dove about Peter, Tink had felt different. Her limbs were looser. Her chest was more open. Her mind was extraordinarily sharp. She even managed to think of more Peter stories, funny ones that lightened the look in Mother Dove's eyes, if just for a moment.

But as night fell, Mother Dove seemed to stop listening. Her head tilted oddly, and when she fell asleep, her breathing was more laboured than it had been the night before. Each exhale rattled, and her whole frame trembled. Tink listened and feared that each breath would be the last.

Only two days earlier, the hawk would have heard the fairies before they came close. But now he heard nothing.

They advanced slowly, eighteen brave inches forward, twelve frightened inches back. Finally, they were within a yard of him. He didn't move.

"He doesn't look golden," Prilla whispered. He looked brown.

"It would be idiotic to be eaten by the wrong hawk, darlings."

The hawk ruffled his feathers, showing glints of gold.

"Rani, sweetheart, who will pluck – "

" – him?" Rani knew she couldn't pluck a live bird, even for a good reason. Vidia, with her plucking experience, was the logical choice. But Rani didn't want to send her into danger alone.

Rani drew Tink's dagger. "Vidia, you'll pluck the feather. I'll fly to his stomach. If he tries to attack, I'll stab him. Prilla, you'll hover around his head. Pull down his eyelids or something, but stay away from his beak."

How will I do that? Prilla wondered. But she didn't complain. Maybe, she thought, my talent is for avoiding beaks. She took her place, her wings fluttering double-time with fear.

Rani positioned herself at the hawk's stomach. Vidia touched a wing feather. The hawk didn't feel Vidia, but he felt a bit of warmth at his belly and near his face.

Vidia pulled. The hawk's head jerked up. Someone was trying to kill him! He had one defence left, a single magic power. He shared his pain.

A bolt of pain surged up Vidia's arms. She hung on even though the pain mounted. The feather wouldn't come out. She gritted her teeth and tugged harder. It began to give. She yanked with all her strength.

Remember the worst pain you've ever felt. Close your eyes and think of it. Perhaps Vidia's and the hawk's pain was less than yours. Perhaps more. But it was the worst either of them had ever felt.

They screamed so piercingly that a star flickered.

Then the pain receded, and Vidia had the feather. The fairies flew away as fast as they could.

Prilla called back, "Thank you, Mr. Golden Hawk!"

He didn't hear. He swayed on his stone, dizzy from the plucking.

Vidia soon outpaced the others.

She could have acknowledged then and there how much plucking hurt. She could have admitted she'd been cruel to pluck Mother Dove. She could have recognised that pain is pain, whether it's pain to others or pain to oneself. She could have sworn not to inflict pain on purpose ever again.

But instead, she convinced herself that the hawk was the one who'd been cruel. She decided he'd made the pain worse than it really was.

It was almost dawn when the questers arrived at the fairy circle.

Vidia took out the feather, which she had tucked into her blouse.

Rani and Prilla came to look. The topside of the feather was brown, but the underside was gold. Prilla touched it. It felt metallic and cold.

Vidia deposited the feather next to the egg and the cigar holder. The three fairies curled up in the shed, where no hawks would come.

Prilla thought, We succeeded twice. Maybe we can save Mother Dove.

Before she fell asleep, she tried once more to transport herself to the mainland. She closed her eyes and pictured herself in the tunnel again. She pictured the mainland at the far end. She flew along, imagining a Clumsy girl in a bed, hugging a stuffed walrus.

She landed on a real girl's pillow.

This girl was hugging a stuffed pelican. She opened her eyes and said, "Do you know how much thirty-five times nine-point-four is?"

Prilla shook her head, wishing she were a mathematics-talent fairy. Even on the mainland, she was disappointing.

TWENTY-THREE

*I*N THE MORNING, there was frost on the ground around the hawthorn. Mother Dove felt old, a thousand years old. Tink began to feed her breakfast to her, spoonful by spoonful.

After a few bites, Mother Dove said, "Put it aside."

"Just three more spoonfuls."

Mother Dove accepted them. Tink's nursing had improved. Wonders never ceased. In the midst of everything terrible, they never ceased.

When they emerged from the shed, the questers found that a basket of food had been left for them. There was also a note from Queen Ree.

> *I am so proud of you for achieving your second goal.*
> *Our thoughts are always with you.*

The queen is proud of me, Prilla thought, even if I don't have a talent. Me! And I'm only four days old. She did a handstand.

Rani smiled at her. Prilla caught the smile and grinned back.

After breakfast, the questers flew to the lagoon. Rani kept trying to think of a way to get the mermaids' attention.

You see, the hard truth about Never mermaids is that they're snobs. If you don't have a green tail and a siren's voice, you're not worth bothering with.

They have no use for fairies, or for most Clumsies, although they like Peter. After all, he's the Peter, which has snob appeal. And he's so good at pretending to have a tail that the mermaids can actually see it.

Mermaids always dive when fairies approach. Laughing, they swim to their castle under the sea.

This castle is as delicate as a goldfish skeleton. It lacks walls, and you can see from the dining room clear to the servants' quarters.

There is one walled room, however, and it is the mermaids' secret shame. The room holds no water, only air. You see, Never mermaids cannot go on forever without air. Eventually their gills tire. If they prefer not to rise to the surface, they visit the wind room, as they call it.

When the questers reached the lagoon's beach, they could just barely make out two mermaids sunning on Marooners' Rock. The two were gossiping in Mermish, a language with thirty-eight vowels and no consonants. When they want to, however, mermaids can understand and speak to fairies and Clumsies.

Vidia said, "Loves, they'll dive if we go – "

" – to them. But what else can we do?"

Prilla wished she had a talent for mermaids.

"Dear heart, we need a note."

Rani nodded. A note was a good idea. The mermaids might read a note.

But they had nothing to write on, and nothing to write with.

Vidia said she'd get a note from Ree. "I'll be back before you – "

" – think."

" – blink." She flew off.

Rani said to Prilla, "Let's try to talk to them anyway."

They flew out over the lagoon. Rani touched Prilla's arm, and they stopped just beyond where the mermaids would notice them.

Prilla gasped in astonishment.

Think of flute music. Think of the scent of pine needles. Think of ice-cold lemonade sparkling down your throat. Now you have it – mermaids.

Rani watched a mermaid dribble water on her face. She

watched another dive, deep, deep. She watched one laugh as a wave lapped over her head. Oh, to feel a wave!

Prilla watched three mermaids bat a huge bubble about with their heads and their tails. Oh, to fly over and join their game!

She and Rani resumed flying. Rani shouted, "Help! Don't dive!"

The mermaids dived.

Rani and Prilla headed back to shore.

Prilla said, "They'll read the note. They probably don't get letters very often."

They reached the beach just as Vidia returned with Ree's note, written on linen in colorfast raspberry ink.

Dear mermaids, please give my fairies a comb, which we need to bring back Neverland's magic. Many thanks from the queen of the fairies.

They looked for something to weigh down the note. Mermaids love pretty things, so they looked for something pretty. After a few minutes, Prilla spotted a glittery blue rock sticking out of the sand.

The fairies wrapped the note around the rock and tied it with the yellow ribbon Vidia had brought back with her.

Then the three of them lightened the package with fairy dust and carried it out to sea with them. When they reached the spot where the mermaids had been playing, they let it go.

They flew back to shore to wait. Rani sat and stared out to sea, thinking of Mother Dove. Vidia paced in the air, thinking of Mother Dove's feathers.

Prilla began to build a sand castle.

She was at a beach on the mainland. She flew here and there, observing Clumsy children's sand castle–building techniques.

Back on Neverland, she knew what her castle needed – wet sand. She went down to the ocean's edge.

"Dear child, if you get your wings wet, you'll be completely useless."

Prilla retreated from the water. She knew Vidia was right, but she wished Vidia didn't have such a talent for making her feel stupid.

Mother Dove's legs felt all pins and needles. She rose to shift her position, but her legs gave out. She collapsed with a squeak.

Tink didn't know what to do. She wasn't strong enough to lift Mother Dove into a more comfortable spot. And she didn't have any more stories to tell.

But then she thought of her finger harp. She took it out of her skirt pocket. Her fingers wanted to play a dirge, but she forced them to pick out Mother Dove's favourite tune, "Fairy Dust Melody."

Mother Dove clung to the thread of music and closed her mind to her broken body and her ruined egg.

Two hours passed, and the mermaids didn't surface. The questers began to lose hope.

They didn't know it, but the mermaids weren't being snobby this time. They simply misunderstood, and one can hardly blame them.

Imagine you're a mermaid. A wrapped package drops down to you, tied with a ribbon. Which do you focus on? The wrapper? Or what's inside the wrapper?

It never occurred to the mermaids to examine the wrapper. They untied the ribbon and saw the pretty blue stone. They admired it and passed it from one to another. Then they brought it to their treasure room.

The note wound up on the ocean floor, where a starfish used it as a blanket.

On shore, Prilla said, "Too bad we can't go down there and make them listen." She wished she had a shouting-through-water talent.

Prilla's remark gave Rani an idea.

"Sweethearts, let's stop wasting – "

" – time. Hush, Vidia. I'm thinking." Rani considered her idea. Could she do it? Could she make the sacrifice? She tried to think of another way.

More time passed. No mermaids. Rani couldn't think of another way.

She took out Tink's dagger and began to weep. She handed the dagger to Vidia. "I'll dive to the mermaids. I'll beg them for a comb. Cut off my wings."

TWENTY-FOUR

VIDIA TOOK the dagger. "You'd cut off your wings?" For once her tone wasn't mocking.

Rani nodded bravely. "I've always wanted to swim."

Vidia would have died rather than given up her wings. She said, "Pet, they still may not give you a comb."

"You'll have lost your wings for nothing." Prilla wrung her hands. This was much worse than the hawk or the pirate.

Rani yelled, "Don't tell me what I already know!"

Prilla wanted to say she'd give up her wings so Rani wouldn't have to, but the words wouldn't come. Instead, she said, "Won't it – "

" – hurt? It doesn't hurt."

Prilla really knew this. She just wasn't thinking. Wings don't hurt. Cutting off a Never fairy's wing is no more painful than cutting hair.

Vidia raised the dagger. And lowered it. Raised it again, and lowered it again. She couldn't do it. She was a fast-flier, and she couldn't cut anyone's wings off. She held the knife out to Prilla. "You do it, dear child."

"Me? Oh, no! Not me."

"Vidia..."

"Can't do it, love. Can't."

"Prilla," Rani said, "cut them off."

Prilla shook her head.

"Do it. I command you to."

Prilla took the dagger. She was crying so hard she could barely see. She held a wing just above where it met Rani's shoulder blade. She made a nick and jumped back.

"That's it," Rani said. "Keep going."

Prilla sawed at what looked like a short tree branch with the bark peeled off. To her relief it didn't bleed. It was dense, though, and cutting through it was slow going.

Vidia couldn't stand to watch, so she rose into the air and began to fly along the shore.

Rani called after her, "Get the carrier." They'd need it to bring her and the comb back to land. "Keep going, Prilla."

Prilla was making good progress now. "I hope I don't have a talent for cutting off – "

" – wings." Rani laughed through her tears. "Wait." She turned and hugged a surprised Prilla. "You have a talent for being sweet." She turned back. "Keep cutting."

If Prilla could have cried harder, she would have. No one had ever hugged her before. After a minute she said, "Is there really a talent for being sweet?"

"No, but there should be."

Oh, Prilla thought. Oh, well.

At last the first wing was off. The second went quicker because Prilla had gotten the hang of it. The wing came off and plopped on the sand. The wing slits of Rani's dress hung open. Her wing stumps were milky white. Their surface was rough, with tiny sharp points sticking up.

"Thank you, Prilla." Rani couldn't look at the discarded wings. She went to the water and waded in up to her waist. She'd never dared go so far in before. The water soothed her.

Prilla thought the wings didn't look as if they'd ever had anything to do with flight. They were just bony frames wrapped in gauze.

But wait! They began to change. The frames turned from dull white to glossy pink.

"Rani, look!" Prilla shouted.

Rani hurried out of the water, frightened at Prilla's tone.

The wings began to vibrate. Rani wondered if they were going to disappear.

The vibrating stopped. Diamond chips and tiny aquamarines shimmered through the gauze.

"They're beautiful," Prilla breathed.

Rani felt better. She must have done the right thing for her wings to become so marvellous.

Vidia landed with the balloon carrier. "What are those pretties?"

A note of pride crept into Rani's voice. "My wings." She stood up straight. "Now, take me to the mermaids."

"We have to put the wings somewhere safe." Prilla carried them and Rani's boots to a jumble of driftwood. She placed everything carefully out of the wind.

Rani gave the satchel of dust to Prilla. Then she sat in the carrier, and Prilla pulled her out over the water while Vidia flew ahead. When they neared Marooners' Rock, Rani jumped into the sea.

She went under, and her dream of being surrounded by water came true. She wriggled her toes, flexed her fingers, curled herself into a ball, straightened herself out. She took great underwater leaps with her arms spread out.

She opened her eyes. Big fish and small fish swam by. Gaily colored fish and drab fish and almost transparent fish swam by. A sea horse just Rani's size rocked by.

She was running out of air. She didn't know how to swim, but she had an instinct for it. She moved her arms in a breaststroke and her legs in a scissors kick. In a few seconds she broke the surface of the water.

Vidia and Prilla hovered above her. She waved, took a deep breath, and dived back under.

TWENTY-FIVE

R ANI DESCENDED toward an upturned face. A
mermaid!

This mermaid was called Soop by Peter Pan, since he
couldn't pronounce her real name.

Mermaids aren't curious about other creatures. Ordinarily,
Soop would have swum away from Rani. But she had
quarrelled with her best friend, and she was looking for
amusement. She held out her hand for Rani to land on.

The hand was longer than a Clumsy's hand, long enough to
be useful as a flipper, and the fingernails were wee fins. Soop
was as big as a Clumsy, but not clumsy in the slightest. She
was as graceful as the long pink scarf that swirled around her.

Soop wasn't sure if Rani was a wingless fairy, or a new
creature entirely. She brought Rani up close to her face.

Rani was surprised to see that the mermaid's skin was made
up of tiny glistening scales.

Soop gently turned Rani around. She saw Rani's wing
stumps and realised what Rani had done.

The realisation broke through Soop's snobbiness. She
could imagine only one explanation for the sacrifice: this
fairy had cut off her wings so she could swim with mermaids.

Soop wept briefly, although Rani couldn't tell. She bowed her head, and Rani saw the comb nestled in the flowing yellow-green hair.

The comb was made of whalebone. The teeth were fashioned into a toothy grin. The handle was in the shape of a shark's body, set with four enormous pearls.

Soop said, "Welcome, little fairy." The words reverberated strangely in the water.

Rani caught the word *fairy* and assumed the rest was a greeting. She couldn't speak, so she smiled. A curtsy would have been appreciated, but Prilla was the only fairy to know about curtsies.

Soop pointed out the castle and gardens.

Rani was running out of air. She extended her arms in an imploring gesture. She pretended to comb her hair and then stretched her arms out again.

Soop said politely, "Your hair is nice too."

Rani had to have air soon. She pretended to take a comb out of her hair and give it to Soop. She hoped Soop would get the hint.

But Soop just thought the fairy had scratched her head.

Rani's face turned red. Soop understood that the fairy needed air. She cupped her hands around Rani and started for the wind room.

Rani tried to get free. Her lungs were bursting. She hesitated, then kicked Soop's hand.

"I'm trying to help, foolish fairy." Soop swam through the arched entry to the castle.

Rani couldn't see through Soop's fingers, but I'll tell you what she missed.

A mermaid swept back and forth on a seaweed swing. Three laughing mermaids chased a Never scurry fish. A merman and a mermaid sang a duet.

Soop concealed her hands under her scarf. The fairy was her secret.

Rani's ears were pounding, and she thought her lungs were going to explode. She kept kicking Soop's fingers, but her kicks were growing weaker.

Soop rose to the castle's second story. Rani kicked once more before losing consciousness.

"What should we do?" Prilla had started holding her breath when Rani went under, and she'd run out of air at least two minutes ago.

"Dear child, don't ask me. I'm not the leader."

Several more minutes passed.

Vidia said, "I'm leaving, dear child."

"Please don't go."

Vidia started to fly away. "Farewell, dear child."

For the first time in her life, Prilla felt rage. "Dear *old hag*, if Rani gets the comb, the quest will fail because of you."

Vidia turned. "Dear child, Rani is dead."

"Maybe not. We don't know what's down there."

"And why will the quest fail because of me?"

"Because I can't get a comb and Rani on the carrier by myself."

Vidia hadn't thought of that. She said it was pointless, but she agreed to wait for half an hour.

Prilla stared down into the water. She thought, Please don't be dead, Rani.

In the wind room, Rani lay still in Soop's hand. Soop wondered if the fairy was dead. There'd be no amusement in a dead fairy. She poked Rani's stomach. "Wake up, fairy."

Rani gagged. Water streamed out of her mouth and nose. She coughed and began to breathe.

But the stink made her wish she were still unconscious. The wind room reeked of fish!

Mother Dove had closed her eyes, but Tink didn't think she was asleep. Mother Dove kept squeezing her eyes shut, and every few minutes a muscle in her cheek jumped.

It's pain, Tink thought. She wished she could do something, but there was nothing to do. She started "Fairy Dust Melody" again on her harp. She intended to keep playing it, even though she had blisters on all her fingers. If her fingers gave out, she'd play with her toes.

Now that she had air, Rani was able to explain her mission.

Soop could imagine what losing their flight and their magic would mean to the fairies. And she was willing to give away her comb. She had lots of combs.

But she wanted something in return. "If I give you a present, you must give me a – "

" – present." Rani wished she'd brought something with her. "I'll give you my belt." It wasn't much, but it was all she had. It was a fine belt, made of woven beetle hair.

"Not that. Although it's very pretty. I want..." What did she want? Hmm...Yes! "I want a magic wand."

Oh, no! Rani thought. "Never fairies don't have magic wands."

Soop was puzzled. "Fairies don't have magic wands?"

"We don't. Great Wanded fairies do, and some others."

"So you will get me a magic wand from them. I will wait." She took the comb out of her hair.

Rani accepted it. They'd worry about the wand later. She

thanked Soop and left, pushing the comb ahead of her. Vidia and Prilla probably thought she'd drowned by now. She hoped they were still waiting.

They were arguing about whether or not half an hour had gone by. Prilla turned a cartwheel when she saw Rani.

It did take both Prilla and Vidia to lift the comb onto the carrier and help Rani climb in. When they reached shore, they retrieved Rani's boots and wings.

At the fairy circle, they loaded the egg and the cigar holder onto the carrier. Rani laid the golden feather in the bottom. She could have left her wings behind, but she wanted them nearby. She sat down in the carrier and cradled them in her arms. Prilla added the loaves of bread that had been placed in the shed for them.

Vidia said, "Hurry up, dear child. Mustn't keep a dragon waiting."

Prilla picked up the balloon carrier cord and began to fly, pulling Rani and the quest items behind her. She wondered if Kyto could be wicked enough to refuse the things they were bringing him, even if he wanted them. Would he want even more for the animals and Clumsies of Neverland to age and die? Would he want the fairies to run out of fairy dust?

Could any creature be wicked enough to want Mother Dove to die?

TWENTY-SIX

*T*HE BALLOON CARRIER was almost too heavy to fly. It couldn't rise higher than a few inches, and sometimes it bumped over tree stumps and large rocks.

The day's fairy dust ran out soon after the questers crossed the Wough River. Night had fallen, and Rani, who was giving orders quite naturally now, said they'd stop until morning.

A dusting of snow fell overnight. When Ree saw the snow, she was aghast. The island looked beautiful, but what would happen if two inches fell? Snow would be up to the fairies' waists. Six inches, and they'd be buried.

In the underground home, Peter Pan's blanket was halfway down his chest. He pulled it up and exposed his feet and ankles. He stood, and his head grazed the ceiling. He'd grown seven inches overnight.

Captain Hook ripped the leg off his stateroom table to use as a cane.

The Never bear wanted to go fishing, but he couldn't remember where Havendish Stream was.

To Tink's surprise, Mother Dove looked better, less tense around the eyes. She felt better, too. She felt cold and old, but not so ill.

She sensed that the egg was on its way to Kyto. Her body began to repair itself in anticipation of the egg's return.

"I'm hungry." Mother Dove hadn't thought she'd ever be hungry again.

Tink wanted to hug Mother Dove, but she was afraid of hurting her. Instead, she said, "I'll bring breakfast, lots of breakfast. It'll be delicious." She shouted to Nilsa, the scout hovering above them, "I'll be back soon. With breakfast!"

Nilsa, who'd eaten only once since the hurricane, yelled, "Good."

Tink ran-flew across the open beach, while keeping an eye out for hawks. She hurried to Fairy Haven. She expected to return in no time, but she didn't realise that, without dust, the kitchen would be very slow.

When the questers awoke, they found themselves on the edge of a vast prairie. A small triangle on the horizon was Torth Mountain, where Kyto was imprisoned.

Rani sprinkled only a quarter cup of the final day's dust on Vidia and Prilla, and none on herself, since she couldn't fly.

Vidia was furious. "Give me a full ration, dearie." She

reached out for the satchel.

"No," Rani said, backing away. "I'll sprinkle on more if we run out before we get to Kyto. But if we make it, and he doesn't fix the egg, we'll walk home and save – "

Vidia lunged and got a hand on the satchel. Rani hung on. Prilla jumped up and down, not knowing what to do.

Rani caught Vidia's eye and held it. "Ree made me leader, and I won't let her down."

After a tense minute, Vidia let go. "Honey lamb, whatever happens with Kyto, I'll expect my share of dust. And, my sweet, I'll get it."

An hour went by before Tink left Fairy Haven with breakfast. When she reached the beach, a fox was stalking Mother Dove.

Mother Dove was standing, swaying, and trying to back away.

Tink dropped the food and raced toward the fox, all the while wondering where that miserable scout Nilsa had gone.

Mother Dove called to Tink to get away and save herself. Tink yelled at the fox, telling him to leave, warning him not to hurt Mother Dove, promising him something else to eat.

He was too hungry to listen. He was five yards from Mother Dove.

She raised her broken wings.

Tink shouted, "Fly, Mother Dove! Fly!"

Mother Dove flapped her wings once.

Tink threw herself onto the fox's right front leg. He snapped at her, but missed.

Mother Dove flapped her wings again. The fox advanced a yard.

Tink climbed up his leg, grasping fistfuls of fur.

He was three yards from Mother Dove.

Mother Dove rose an inch into the air.

Tink was almost at the fox's shoulder.

Mother Dove collapsed in the sand. The fox was two yards away. Tink climbed onto his head.

One yard.

Tink drew out her dagger.

He reached Mother Dove.

Tink heard a snap.

Mother Dove screamed.

Tink stuck her legs into the fox's ear and pushed down.

He yelped and shook his head.

Tink fell out and down, beating the air with her wings. It was a long drop. She broke a leg, but didn't feel it.

The fox leaned down to finish her off. But before he could, she thrust her dagger deep into his neck. She saw blood, and he stumbled away, yowling with pain.

Mother Dove's shoulder was bleeding heavily. "Nilsa died..." Mother Dove lost her breath.

"Why didn't she fly out of reach?"

"...of disbelief."

The scout had died before the fox had come. It had been terrible for Mother Dove to watch Nilsa's anguished fading, unable to do a thing.

Why did I have to go for breakfast? Tink thought.

"Don't blame yourself," Mother Dove whispered. "You rescued me." She tried to hold back a groan, but it got out.

Tink blamed herself nonetheless.

And now she was going to leave again, to find Beck, who might know how to stop Mother Dove's bleeding. She hurried to Fairy Haven, almost at a full run, ignoring her broken leg.

But while she ran, she wondered if she should have stayed. What if Mother Dove died while she was gone – died all alone?

TWENTY-SEVEN

*T*erence sprinkled enough fairy dust on Beck so she could fly to Mother Dove. A nursing-talent fairy set Tink's leg while Terence looked on, wincing. Ree questioned Tink about what had happened.

On the beach, Beck cleaned Mother Dove's wound with soapy dew and pressed moss into it to staunch the bleeding. The injury was very bad.

Mother Dove whispered, "Don't cry, Beck."

How could she not cry? She doubted even the egg could save Mother Dove.

The questers flew along the prairie, through a field of raindrop cactus and by a herd of curly-maned horses. After three hours they reached the hills leading to Torth Mountain. An hour more, and they began to fly over the mountain's lower slopes. Vidia, in the lead as always, saw smoke coming from one of the caves. Kyto's cave.

Tink, limping on crutches, accompanied Ree to the beach to see how Mother Dove was faring.

Beck just shook her head.

The questers ran out of dust at noon, with several caves in sight above them. It would take about an hour of flying to reach them.

Prilla was thrilled. They were almost there, and they'd come so far. It had been such an adventure, and she'd been part of it. She'd escaped from Hook, and she'd persuaded Vidia to wait for Rani. Even with no talent, she'd helped.

Rani said they should eat lunch before going on. Prilla was too excited to eat. She jumped up and tried to turn a cartwheel, which was hard without fairy dust. Her wings overbalanced her, and she fell against the carrier.

Rani laughed. Prilla's high jinks made her forget her wings, sometimes. She finished her bread and brushed the crumbs off her dress.

Prilla did a split and a handspring. Rani stood and pulled the dust satchel strap over her head. Prilla tried again to do a cartwheel. Rani opened the dust satchel just as Prilla crashed into her. Rani tumbled backward and spilled the remaining fairy dust into the wind.

Mother Dove developed a fever. Her beak chattered, and her eyes were too bright. Beck built up the sand around her and over her back to warm her. Tink hopped here and there, pressing down to make her snug.

Mother Dove thought she didn't mind dying so much. But she minded never learning if her egg had been saved.

She thought of telling Ree that the time had come to pluck her.

Soon. She'd tell Ree soon. In the meanwhile she'd try to hang on a little longer.

No one was speaking to Prilla. Vidia had actually slapped her when the dust blew away.

Prilla had said she was sorry.

Rani had answered, "Clumsies say they're sorry. Fairies say *I'd fly backward if I could*."

So Prilla had said, "I'd fly backward if I could."

But no one had answered.

Prilla wasn't talking to herself either, except to call herself names. She'd ruined everything. That was her talent. Even if Kyto fixed the egg, Mother Dove would probably be dead before they got back to Fairy Haven.

Rani was sure there was no point to going on. But she led them on anyway.

They climbed on foot. Luckily they didn't have to carry the carrier, because its balloons still had dust.

As they climbed, they watched for hawks. Vidia thought again of sharing her fresh dust. She had enough to fly herself and Prilla to Kyto and home again. But if he didn't restore the egg, she wanted to keep the dust, the last dust anyone would ever have.

Mother Dove was delirious.

She was back in her mama's nest, waiting anxiously for food. She was playing with her sisters and brothers, pecking them and being pecked. She was poised at the edge of the nest, working up courage for her first flight.

Tink was almost knocked over as Mother Dove tried to fly. Her wounded shoulder and broken wings should have hurt terribly, but Mother Dove's mind was too far in the past to feel the pain.

TWENTY-EIGHT

*I*N FOUR hours the questers reached the first cave, which was uninhabited.

Prilla heard low snap-crackling. After a few minutes, Rani and Vidia heard it too. Fire! Kyto!

And Kyto heard them. Fairies don't make much noise, especially when they're barely speaking to each other. But they breathe. He heard their breathing.

They climbed a crack in the rock leading to his cave. The temperature rose as they climbed. Rani was dripping sweat, and all her leafkerchiefs were soaked.

Halfway up, Kyto's smell reached them, and they almost fell off the mountain. He stank of hundreds of years without a bath or a toothbrush.

The fairies peeked over the rim of his ledge. He saw their wide-eyed faces. The balloon carrier bobbed a few inches above the ledge.

Prilla would have felt sorry for him if his face hadn't been so cruel. He was the size of a small elephant, and she doubted he had enough room even to turn around. His skin was scarred and chafed from pressing against his bars.

At second glance Prilla saw they weren't bars. He was confined by roots, Never Bimbim tree roots, which dropped over the cave opening and anchored themselves in the rock at the cave's edge. These remarkable roots are impervious to fire, and the more they're pushed against, the more they resist.

Although Prilla couldn't tell, Kyto didn't quite fill his cave. There was room in the back for his meagre hoard.

A Never raven flew by, about ten feet from the cave. Kyto exhaled fire and roasted the bird in the air. Then he inhaled powerfully and sucked it to him. It stuck in the roots, but he yanked it through with his teeth and ate it whole.

Rani thought, He'll cook us before we say a word!

Prilla wished she had a talent for dragons. If only she knew how to tame him!

He glared at them. "Go away, unless you've come to free me." His voice was low and raspy from smoldering for six hundred years.

The questers exchanged frightened glances. Finally, Rani found her voice. "We c-can't f-free you. We're n-not strong enough."

"Then go away."

The fairies ducked just in time. A jet of fire barely missed Prilla's ear.

Rani had to calm herself before she could find her voice again. "We've c-come to t-trade. If you help us, we'll give you three things for your hoard. B-beautiful things."

"Show them to me."

Rani reached for the balloon carrier.

"Dearest," Vidia hissed, "don't be a fool. He'll inhale – "

" – them." Rani nodded. "Er, I'll d-describe them, K-Kyto."

He hid his excitement when she was through. There were only two golden hawk feathers in dragon hoards anywhere. His would be the third. Double cigar holders and mermaid's combs were rare too. His hoard would finally join the top rank of dragon hoards.

"Give them to me, and I won't eat you."

The questers ducked below the ledge.

Rani called out, "D-don't eat us!'

"Then give them to me!"

"N-not unless you help us," Prilla called.

Rani said, "We'll t-take the things b-back home and stop b-bothering you." She paused, then added, "We'll p-put them on d-display."

Display them! They belonged to him! Kyto belched a ball

of fire. "What do you want?"

Rani stammered her way through telling him about Mother Dove and the egg.

"Show me this egg."

They had to stand on the ledge to do it. Terrified, Prilla and Rani climbed up.

Kyto noticed that Rani had no wings.

Vidia reached into the carrier and lifted the egg onto the ledge. She started to climb up, but thought better of it. If he flamed, let the others get crisped.

As soon as Kyto saw the egg, he knew he could restore it. He pretended to consider.

Please, Prilla thought, please be able to do it. Please save Mother Dove. Please don't kill us.

"Give me the things for my hoard..." Flames played around his lips. "...and I'll fix your – "

" – egg." Rani said she'd give him one hoard item immediately. Then, after he had restored the egg, she'd give him the other two. "Which do you want first?"

"The feather."

Vidia looked for it in the carrier, but she didn't see it. She moved things aside and still didn't see it. "Where..."

Prilla and Rani climbed down and helped her look. No feather.

"It must have blown out," Rani whispered.

Kyto heard. He was enraged. Bumbling fairies! He sent a fireball over the ledge where they were. It missed them by inches and singed Prilla's hair.

It took several minutes before Rani recovered enough to speak. "We still have the c-comb and the cigar holder."

"Three items. You said three items."

"Please, Mr. Kyto," Prilla begged. "Mother Dove needs her egg."

He didn't answer. He didn't care if Mother Dove lived or died.

Rani wiped the sweat off her nose. "We do have something else." She picked up her wings and held them to her chest. "Something more extraordinary than a golden feather. A pair of jewelled fairy wings."

TWENTY-NINE

"RANI, DON'T do it!" Prilla cried.

Fairy wings? Kyto was thrilled. With fairy wings, his hoard would be unique. "Let me see."

"You can't have them!" Prilla yelled.

Kyto got ready to blow another fireball.

"Hush, Prilla." Rani told Kyto, "You can't see them yet, but I'll tell you about them." It would be a magnificent end for them, if they turned out to be the wings that saved Mother Dove. She described them.

He listened greedily. Real wings from a real fairy who'd never fly again.

Kyto wanted the wings first, but Rani refused. She'd give him the double cigar holder. Then, after he restored the egg, he could have the comb and the wings.

He smiled to himself. The fairies were so trusting. In their place, he'd have made sure Mother Dove was well before he'd

FAIRY DUST AND THE QUEST FOR THE EGG

given away the final item.

Prilla and Rani dragged the cigar holder up to the cave and ran away.

He ran a claw over the holder. He rubbed his cheek along it. He sniffed it and licked it. He wished the fairies would leave and give him a few hours alone with it.

But Prilla carried the egg to him. Its pale blue shell had black splotches. The two smaller pieces nested in the big one. Atop them were the ashes that had been the egg.

Prilla rushed back to the edge of the cliff and stood next to Rani, watching. Kyto exhaled a golden flame that spat and sizzled. Through the flame, the fairies could make out the eggshell, which wasn't changing a bit.

Kyto swallowed his flame. "This is more difficult than I expected." He frowned. "I hope I can do it." Inside himself he laughed. Dragons are show-offs, and he was having fun.

Prilla wanted to scold the egg, tell it this was its last chance and couldn't it cooperate?

Kyto blew a red flame, deep as a raspberry, bright as a tomato. It rustled and crackled as it played over, around, and through the eggshell, which remained stubbornly broken.

Rani wiped her wet face. Had she sacrificed her wings for nothing?

Kyto let the flame subside. "Fairies, I will make one more

140

attempt."

He heaved forth a midnight-blue flame that hurled out miniature lightning bolts. A wind ripped across the ledge. Rani and Prilla threw themselves on the ground. Vidia ducked.

Prilla raised her head to watch, but the egg was hidden in flame. Kyto's cheeks were puffed out, his eyes protruded, and his whole body strained toward the egg.

His flame licked a low-lying cloud. The heat scorched a sparrow flying two miles away. Three miles away a field of grass caught fire.

At that moment, Kyto spat into the restored yolk. Then he repaired the shell, leaving a gob of his wickedness inside.

The flame withdrew. There was the egg, whole again.

Mother Dove sank into a deep sleep. All the fairies gathered around her. If she awoke before she died, they wanted to be there to tell her farewell.

The burn marks were gone from the egg. It was the same pale blue it used to be. Rani touched it, and it felt smooth and cool. She was sure it was perfect.

Prilla and Rani carried the comb to Kyto. Then Rani brought over her wings and gave them a final pat.

Kyto could have crisped the fairies, now that he'd gotten

what he wanted. But if he did, no one would know the trick he'd played on the egg. So he let them go.

Rani and Prilla loaded the egg into the balloon carrier while Vidia steadied the carrier. The three of them started down the mountain. It would take them more than a week to walk home. Mother Dove would probably be dead by then.

Prilla was beside herself with misery. We did everything, she thought. But it may all be useless, just because I had to turn a cartwheel.

Vidia was arguing furiously with herself. If she shared her fresh dust, they might reach Mother Dove in time. But if Mother Dove didn't recover, Vidia would have wasted the last of her dust, and she'd never fly again.

On the other hand, she had only about two days of dust left. Which should she choose: the certainty of those two days or the chance of flying forever?

"Um, darlings, actually we can fly home. I have – "

" – dust. Dust! Dust?"

Vidia nodded.

Prilla and Rani stared. She'd had dust with her all along?

Prilla thought, At least I don't have a talent for being a selfish pig.

Mother Dove soared above the beach where her body lay

inert. She was still attached to that body. But the string that held her was thinning, and soon it would snap.

A music-talent fairy began the fairies' saddest song, "Fly Not Far from Me." More voices joined her, one by one.

Rani sat in the balloon carrier. Vidia sprinkled her dust on Prilla and on herself. Prilla noticed the difference instantly. With the fresh dust she felt weightless, and her wings felt as strong as an eagle's wings. She understood the temptation to pluck Mother Dove – not that she'd ever do it.

But although they were able to travel faster than they had before, it still took two and a half hours to reach the Wough River.

Mother Dove was minutes from death. They couldn't possibly reach her in time.

Neverland shrank itself again. They'd flown for only ten more minutes before they passed over Fairy Haven. Two minutes later, they landed on the beach.

Mother Dove felt the egg arrive. She found herself back in her body. The pain almost killed her.

Prilla was shocked when she saw Mother Dove. Her feathers had turned a sickly yellow, except at the shoulder where they were bloodstained. Her head hung down, and her cheeks were sunken.

Mother Dove opened her eyes and spoke in a quavery whisper. "Bring the egg closer."

The questers lifted the egg out of the balloon carrier and brought it to her.

No one breathed. No one moved.

Mother Dove cooed.

Prilla got ready to turn a cartwheel.

Mother Dove extended a claw. A dozen fairies rushed in to stop her from toppling.

She moaned, "Kyto spoiled my egg." Her voice ended in the beginning of a death rattle.

THIRTY

MOTHER DOVE can't die! Prilla thought. I have to save her! I have to try! Belief saves fairies. Maybe belief can save Mother Dove.

Prilla imagined herself in a tunnel. The mainland was at the far end. It had to be!

She flew along.

And there she was, at the carousel, flying from one child to the next, shouting above the organ music. "Clap to save Mother Dove! Clap if you believe in Neverland! Clap so the fairies can fly!" She saw two children clap, and then she was gone.

She was in a school auditorium where a play was being performed. She flew from row to row. "Clap to save Mother Dove! Clap to save Neverland!"

She was in a sandbox. "Clap to keep Peter Pan young!" She flew to the swings. "Clap to save Mother Dove!" She flew to the seesaw. "Clap to save Neverland!"

Back on the beach, the egg began to spin, faster and faster.

Mother Dove was still gasping her last gasp.

Prilla was at a birthday party, hovering above the birthday candles. "Clap to save Mother Dove! Clap for Neverland!"

The egg shimmered as it spun. The fairies heard a high whistle. Rani and Vidia heard the crackle of Kyto's flame.

Prilla flew over a line of children watching a parade. "Clap for Mother Dove! Clap for fairies!"

Mother Dove began to shimmer.

Prilla zoomed from home to home, shouting, "Clap! Clap! Clap for Mother Dove! Clap! Clap!"

Clap! if you're reading this. Clap for Mother Dove! Clap for Neverland! Clap for Prilla! Clap!

The fairies heard a faint rustle. The sound grew to a roar. Was it what they thought?

It was! Children were clapping!

The fairies began to shout, "Clap! Clap! Clap for Mother Dove! Clap! Clap!"

The glorious roar grew. Thousands of children clapped. And thousands more.

In the egg, the gob of Kyto's spit dissolved and vanished.

A shudder ran through Neverland.

The clapping stopped, and Prilla returned.

There was Mother Dove, as plump and healthy as she'd been before the hurricane. There was the egg, the good egg, the egg as Kyto should have re-created it, still holding the barest trace of a shimmer.

Prilla blinked, astonished. Then she laughed and turned a cartwheel.

With her wings, Mother Dove cleared sand around the egg. When she was satisfied, she settled herself on top of it.

A warm breeze blew along the beach.

Captain Hook straightened and tossed his table-leg cane overboard.

The Never bear bent his knee experimentally. Why, it was fine!

Peter Pan looked up. The ceiling of the underground home was far above his head. He wasn't growing up! He swore he never would.

The golden hawk rose higher than he'd ever flown before. He spotted a four-leaf clover in the meadow below. He'd never felt better.

On the beach, Mother Dove turned to Tink. "Thank you, Tink. I'll never forget that you cared for me and stood by me through the long, quiet hours. Those were the worst, weren't they?"

Tink nodded.

"You're my champion, Tink."

"We all thank you, Tink," Ree said.

Prilla wondered if Mother Dove was going to thank her.

"Vidia," Mother Dove said, "thank you for going on the quest. I see you've come back unchanged. What a pity."

"Darling, if you really want to thank me, you'll let me pluck a feather or two."

Mother Dove raised her head and whistled, then said, "Rani, Rani. Your poor – "

" – wings."

No one had noticed before, but now Ree cried out, and the other fairies gasped at Rani's empty back.

Rani threw her arms around Mother Dove's neck and sobbed. Then she straightened and said, "I'd do it again."

"I know. I – "

" – know. I swam, Mother Dove. I swam with a mermaid." She turned to Ree. "I promised to give her a magic wand. I had to, or she wouldn't give me her comb."

Ree wondered how they'd keep the promise, but she refused to think about it now.

The fairies heard the beating of wings and looked up in alarm. But it was only another dove, who landed next to Mother Dove.

The two exchanged greetings. Mother Dove said, "This is Brother Dove, Rani. He'll be your wings from now on."

"Oh!" Rani was weeping again.

"Climb on." Brother Dove extended a wing for her to walk up. She did and sat, her legs clamped around his neck.

He chuckled. "I won't let you fall." He rose into the air.

Rani felt as safe as she did flying with her own wings. And she'd never felt flight like this before, so powerful and fast. Oh, so fast! And so high! The fairies were mere specks on the sand below. The ocean was a rich blue, striped with wavy lines of white foam. It was her ocean now. She could play and swim in it and perhaps meet another mermaid.

Brother Dove descended in gradual circles. The fairies applauded as Rani dismounted.

"Whistle when you want me, and I'll come." Brother Dove flew off down the beach.

"And now..." Mother Dove spread her wings and gathered Prilla in.

Prilla felt the softness of Mother Dove's feathers. She inhaled Mother Dove's warm, sweet scent.

Mother Dove released her. Prilla sneezed and smiled dazedly.

"Only Kyto could make the egg whole again," Mother Dove said. "But he contaminated it, and we needed you to make it right. It was a lucky day when you arrived in Neverland." She faced everyone. "Prilla has a new fairy talent. She is our first mainland-visiting clapping-talent fairy."

"Oh. Oh, my!" Prilla thought, I have a talent after all! I haven't been doing anything wrong!

Mother Dove added, "For now, you're the only one in your talent, Prilla. It may be lonely sometimes."

Prilla nodded. So she'd go on being lonely. But it would still be better now that she had a talent.

The fairies were silent. Then Tink said, "Prilla can be an honorary pots-and-pans fairy. We'd be proud to have her."

Prilla turned to Tink in surprise and saw Tink's dimples.

Rani said, "Prilla can be an honorary water-talent fairy. I'll teach her some tricks."

"Thank you, Rani." Prilla was afraid she was going to cry.

Silence fell again.

Then Terence said, "Prilla can be an honorary dust fairy."

Dulcie said, "We'd love for Prilla to be an honorary baker."

Now all the fairies were chiming in, making Prilla a member of their talents.

"Thank you! Thank you!" Prilla wept and turned a dozen somersaults. A dozen cartwheels.

Mother Dove started to tremble. She smiled, utterly happy, and said, "The Molt has begun."